Internal Memo: Jefferson Avenue Firehouse, Courage Bay
From: Chief Dan Egan
To: Captain Joe Ripani
Re: Madison Avenue parking garage collapse

Joe,

I've just finished reading the reports on the collapse of the Madison Avenue parking garage. You and your squad have done it again.

I should have your head for going in there alone the way you did, except I would have done the same myself. Lisa Malloy is alive today because of you, but just think twice before putting your life on the line like that. This job comes with risks on a daily basis, and I can't afford to lose any of my team.

We'll be having a procedural review sometime down the road, when we're not so damn busy with all these follow-up calls. I want all the guys who were on duty for the Madison Avenue collapse to be present. I also want to make sure they know I'm aware of what a great job they've done.

I know you're not one to rest on your laurels, Joe, but a lot of people owe you and your squad a heap of gratitude, and it was your dedicated rescue of Lisa Malloy that stands above the rest.

I may not say it often enough, Joe, but you're one of the best.

About the Author

CODE**RED**

DEBRA WEBB

was born in Scottsboro, Alabama, to parents who taught her that anything is possible if you want it badly enough. She began writing at age nine. Eventually she met and married the man of her dreams, and tried some other occupations, including selling vacuum cleaners and working in a factory, a day-care center, a school, a hospital and a department store.

When her husband joined the military, they moved to Berlin, Germany, and Debra became a secretary in the commanding general's office. By 1985 they were back in the States and moved to Tennessee, to a small town where everyone knows everyone else. For the next five years, Debra worked with NASA's space program at Marshall Space Flight Center in Huntsville, Alabama. Finally, with the support of her family and friends, Debra took up writing again, looking to mystery novels and action-packed movies for her inspiration. In 1998, her dream of writing for Harlequin came true. You can write to Debra at P.O. Box 64, Huntland, Tennessee, 37345, or visit her Web site at www.debrawebb.com to find out exciting news about her next book.

code RED

DEBRA
WEBB

TREMORS

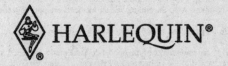

TORONTO • NEW YORK • LONDON
AMSTERDAM • PARIS • SYDNEY • HAMBURG
STOCKHOLM • ATHENS • TOKYO • MILAN • MADRID
PRAGUE • WARSAW • BUDAPEST • AUCKLAND

HARLEQUIN BOOKS
225 Duncan Mill Road, Don Mills,
Ontario, Canada M3B 3K9

ISBN 0-373-61290-7

TREMORS

Copyright © 2004 by Harlequin Books S.A.

Debra Webb is acknowledged as the author of this work

Dear Reader,

The Code Red world is certainly an exciting one! I'm thrilled to be a part of it. I sure hope you'll enjoy Joe and Lisa's story.

Joe Ripani is my favorite kind of hero. A man who will plunge headlong into danger to save a life. A man who stares death in the face and defies the odds. There is only one thing that can strike pure terror in the heart of such a man, and that is love.

Lisa Malloy is a hero, too. She lives a quiet life and devotes her time to healing animals. Safe is all she has ever known. Can she possibly hope to hold her ground where a man like Joe Ripani is concerned?

Follow along on this bumpy road to true love. I think you'll find the ride heartwarming.

Best,

Debra

CHAPTER ONE

THE GROUND TREMBLED.

Captain Joe Ripani of the Courage Bay Fire Department would recall later that it hadn't felt like such a big deal. More like a Magic Fingers bed he remembered from a cheap motel on a family vacation when he'd been a kid. Just a little shimmy as the ancient plates far beneath the Earth's surface groaned and complained and rubbed against each other.

Joe glanced from one member of his squad to the next. Everyone had stopped in the middle of his or her task and taken note of the slight vibration. But no one really looked worried. It was California, after all. A little earthly movement was expected from time to time.

Still, Joe had a bad feeling in his gut. That little tremble telegraphed a tension that crept up his spine, setting off a too-familiar flare of anticipation with each vertebra it climbed. Not good. Salvage, the firehouse's big, black Labrador mascot, apparently had the same feeling. He went still, then whined fretfully.

A full fifteen minutes passed before the true disaster struck.

Jefferson Avenue Firehouse shook as the ground rumbled for an endless thirty seconds. Joe and his crew were already jumping into the necessary gear when the alarm sounded. By the time central dispatch passed on the location, the trucks were rolling out onto the street, sirens wailing.

Traffic on the streets of Courage Bay had come to an abrupt halt, with vehicles sitting haphazardly in the middle of intersections. Pedestrians were still running for cover, though the initial tremor had passed. They all knew that aftershocks could be every bit as lethal as the quake itself. And there would be aftershocks. For days, possibly even weeks, causing nothing more than minor distress, but all the while holding out potential for much, much more.

Joe's fingers tightened around the steering wheel of the firehouse truck. So far, there didn't appear to be too much physical damage. At least not that he could determine from the brief glances he afforded as he cut through the stalled traffic. No reports of fallen buildings, collapsed freeways or overpasses had rattled across the airwaves yet. But that assessment changed when he reached his destination.

The Madison Avenue parking garage had partially collapsed. Joe told himself that at two o'clock in the afternoon, most folks were likely safely tucked away in offices or the various shops that lined the downtown area. Lunch was long over. If he was lucky, the owners of the vehicles parked in the garage wouldn't be anywhere near the collapsed structure.

The instant he skidded to a stop outside the damaged garage, he knew the situation wasn't going to be that simple.

Dozens of pedestrians, co-workers and family members were crying out for help—loved ones or associates were trapped inside the building. A young woman, clearly pregnant, gripped several shopping bags as she frantically tried to explain to a police officer that her mother had gone for the car while she waited in a nearby boutique. Everyone seemed to be talking at once.

Blue lights throbbed and yellow tape fluttered in the breeze as a couple of cops worked to cordon off the area while half a dozen others struggled to hold back the panicked crowd of onlookers.

In the few minutes that had elapsed since the ground shook, Joe knew that a number of things had happened that the average person would not be aware of but would later be grateful for. Rescue resources had been dispatched in response to incoming calls. The first on the scene, whether paramedics, cops or firefighters, had assessed the situation and called for the additional resources needed. With this kind of disaster, the Incident Command System, or ICS, an emergency-management system used to coordinate personnel and equipment resources from multiple agencies, would be put in place.

But Joe had only one concern now. He tuned out the chaos and shouted instructions to his crew. "We'll cover one level at a time."

The parking garage stood four stories, the first of which was completely leveled. Dread pooled in his gut.

Anyone on that level would likely be beyond his help. He said a quick prayer for them and headed into the garage.

"Cap'n, you know we can't go in there until the engineers assess structural integrity." Shannon O'Shea's anticipatory tone belied her warning. "It's not safe."

Joe paused long enough to meet her gaze. "Is it your recommendation that we wait for that resource to arrive?" he demanded. He didn't really need to hear her answer. Shannon, like any good firefighter, was every bit as determined to go in now as he was, but someone had to say the words…had to accept the responsibility for what could happen.

"No, sir," she retorted without hesitation. "I'm prepared to go in now." The other firefighters crowding behind her chimed in with their agreement.

"Let's roll." Joe gave the final authorization.

Conscious of the risk he'd given his squad permission to take, Joe led the way, climbing over the rubble to reach the second level. Slabs of concrete lay upended where T-bars had detached from the outside wall, allowing it to slowly collapse. Time would not be on their side.

"Looks like two and three could go at any minute," O'Shea noted, reaching the same conclusion that he had.

"Yep." Joe didn't slow in his upward movement. There was no time to stop and think. The right side of the second level had dropped several feet, while the entire third floor canted to one side, threatening to give at any second. "Guess that means we'll have to work fast," he said to her with a dim smile. Shannon was good. One of his best. He'd never needed her more than right now.

"And pray," she added, her own movements not slowing.

Dust from the settling debris filtered into his nostrils as he cautiously entered the second level and analyzed the situation. The sound of groaning metal echoed from somewhere. Damaged electrical system, he noted as he moved farther inside. The garage's interior lights would have been helpful, since rubble pretty much blocked the sun. Flashlights clicked on as his team pushed forward, spreading out and cautiously beginning the search for victims trapped in automobiles and beneath fallen debris.

Structural engineers would arrive eventually. What he would give right now for a couple of theodolites to monitor any movement of the building. That very equipment was on order. His team already had the proper training. Without the equipment—he knew the rules— he should wait for approval to enter the structure. But if he waited, people would die. Like that pregnant lady's mother. He couldn't sleep at night with something like that on his conscience.

But what about his squad?

"Damn." The muttered curse echoed across the wireless communications link that kept the squad connected and proved every bit as vital as an umbilical cord. It was the voice of Monte Meyers, known as Bull. "This garage isn't that old. It should have held up better than this."

Joe didn't divert his focus long enough to respond to the remark but he already had his suspicions. California had long ago set into place stringent codes to pre-

vent this very sort of disaster. Even old buildings and
garages were supposed to be retrofitted to meet the new
guidelines. It was the law. And still this kind of devastation could occur. Though it was only conjecture, he
would bet his next paycheck that the garage had, in fact,
been retrofitted. The problem would likely lie in the fact
it had originally been built on a site requiring lots of fill.

He shook his head. The fill would create a base for
construction, but that base would remain soft for many
years, decades maybe. A part of his brain attempted the
math but he couldn't quite recall when the garage had
gone up. The intense shaking caused by the quake as it
spread out from its epicenter had shifted the foundation,
sending concrete pillars and T-bars off center and bringing down tons of concrete atop aluminum and steel vehicles that couldn't possibly support the weight.

"Got one over here!"

The shout came from the other side of the garage.
While two crew members stayed to rescue the victim,
the rest swarmed out like bees searching for a new place
to form a hive. Car after car was visually searched. Inside, underneath. Any void created by fallen rubble
could be protecting trapped victims. In a matter of minutes more than a dozen survivors were found and led
from the unstable site. Others, less fortunate, would be
extracted later.

Joe pointed upward to let those working with him
know that he wanted to head up to level three. It wasn't
necessary to discuss the issue. Their somber expres-
sions said all there was to say. Moving up would add

another layer of peril to the search. Though every man and woman on his crew was physically fit, the combined weight of two or three people could trigger another collapse in such a precarious environment.

But it was a chance they'd have to take.

Judging by the number of victims trapped on level two, there could be that many or more on three. With luck, there would be less. But Joe wouldn't stake anyone's life but his own on luck.

With that in mind, he turned back to his squad. "Let me take it from here." He looked at O'Shea. "You stand ready to bring down anyone I find."

"No way, Cap'n," she said. "I'm going with you."

As much as he'd like to recite all the reasons he felt compelled to do this alone, there was no time. He, better than anyone, knew how stubborn O'Shea could be when it came to her job. Joe heaved a sigh and climbed the last few feet to the next level, O'Shea right on his heels.

Thankfully there weren't as many cars up here as there had been on two. By the time they'd covered one side of the garage, Joe felt fairly confident that this level was clear. And that suddenly looked like the only good luck he would get this day.

He had only half a second's warning.

The screech of strained steel and concrete pierced the air a split second before the far side of level three started to fall.

"Go back!"

Joe shouted the order and hoped everyone heard it over the collapsing tonnage. His frantic gestures to

O'Shea left no question as to his command. She reluctantly retreated, as would the rest of his team on the level below, clambering and sliding down to the safety of the ground amid shattering concrete and flying debris.

By the time he reached the second level there was no place to go except over the side of the structure. He took a moment to ensure that every member of his squad had made it down to the sidewalk before lunging over the side railing himself.

He picked himself up from the ground and dusted off his backside, then winced at the ache in his right side and considered himself lucky that it wasn't worse.

"You okay, Cap'n?" Spike—Sylvester Hilborn—hovered around him like a mother bear. The guy was plenty broad enough to play the part.

"Yeah, I'm okay." He surveyed the group of pedestrians. "Anyone else unaccounted for?"

The Bull shook his head. "Got about a dozen reunions going on over there but no other claims of missing friends or family."

"Good." Joe was thankful for that much, but he couldn't walk away until he knew for certain. Every car that wasn't flattened under rubble had to be inspected. Now. "We'll have to go back in."

Spike nodded. "Crew's standing by. Structural engineers are here." He grimaced. "They're pretty pissed that you went in before they got here."

"I guess they'll just have to get over it." Joe headed toward the two guys in question and didn't bother trying to make nice. They wouldn't be surprised. His reputation usually preceded him. Those who knew him didn't call him the Iceman for nothing. When it came to his job, he always set emotion aside.

It took a full hour to survey the remaining levels. Not a single victim was found. The second level had been cleared before the last collapse, but the third level was questionable. Level four, thankfully, had been deserted. Joe's concern at this point was ensuring that no one on that level had survived and was trapped beneath rubble in a void they hadn't discovered. Sometimes equipment failed. What they needed were the dogs.

That there were no survivors on the first level was pretty much a given; anyone who'd had the misfortune of being in that area was likely dead. Still, they could bring in the dogs and search for remains. It wasn't completely impossible that someone had survived.

"Let's call in the canines and see what we can find." So far, his unit hadn't been asked to respond to any other scene.

"We'll have to wait our turn," Spike informed him. "Apparently there was significant damage on the other side of town. A couple of buildings fell and a church. I heard on the radio that every trained canine in the area has been called in to sniff through the rubble."

Joe shook his head and huffed out a weary breath. Damn, he hated to hear that. He'd hoped, based on what he'd seen and heard en route, that the quake hadn't done that much damage. He should have known better. He'd lived through his share of rumbles.

"Hell," Spike went on, "they said it was so bad on

Poppy Avenue that the church bells actually rang right before the church collapsed."

Courage Bay was not a large city, and Joe's thoughts immediately went to all the people he knew who lived and worked on that side of town.

"Tell 'em we need a dog over here as soon as one is freed up," he said somberly. "Meanwhile, I'm going back in there to see what I can find."

"Cap'n, I think maybe you'd better rethink that strategy," O'Shea said as she walked over. "One of the engineers said the whole backside of level three is down. I doubt there's anything you can do for anyone there now."

"O'Shea, I think I know my job," he said pointedly. She knew the drill. Once the interior of the garage was inspected as fully as possible, the surrounding area was to be rechecked and victims attended to. A command post had already been set up across the street. The EMTs on Joe's crew were taking care of victims. "All I need from you—" he looked from O'Shea to Spike "—is a canine as soon as one comes available."

"With all due respect, sir," O'Shea retorted, not missing a beat, "I'd prefer to join you in the search. Spike here can take care of that call."

She wouldn't like his decision, but Joe wasn't about to risk another life when chances were good that anyone left in the parking garage was already dead.

He would do this alone.

SHE WAS DREAMING of him again.
She knew better…but she dreamed anyway.

Dreamed of making slow, sweet love.

Dreamed of all the fantasies that he'd instilled deep within her heart during their short time together.

Dreamed of picket fences and the pitter-patter of little feet.

Lisa Malloy stirred…the hard facts of reality prodding her from the dreams she so wanted to believe could come true.

But Joe Ripani wasn't a forever kind of guy. He wasn't even a real relationship guy. He was more about instant gratification—grab all you could get before it was too late.

And he definitely wasn't the marrying type…much less the fatherly type.

Lisa moaned softly and tried to surface from what had turned quickly into an unpleasant nightmare.

She wanted to cling to the hope that Joe would somehow morph into the kind of man she longed to spend forever with, but deep inside she knew the truth. Their short affair—and that's the only thing she could call it, since their time together had been spent mainly in his bed—had been all they would ever have. End of subject.

Her head hurt.

Or maybe it was her heart…or both.

She had to wake up. There was a very good reason she shouldn't be sleeping right now.

Something was very, very wrong.

Wake up.

Another groan seeped past her lips. Why couldn't she wake up? Why did her head hurt so badly?

Wake up!

She had to take the first step…had to open her eyes.

"Mmm," she murmured softly. God, what was that pounding in her skull?

Lisa's eyes fluttered open, seemingly of their own accord, since she didn't appear to possess the necessary strength to lift those incredibly heavy lids.

She never took afternoon naps.

What was wrong with her?

Surely this wasn't another symptom of…

Her gaze focused on something in front of her, drawing her full attention in that direction.

Steering wheel.

Windshield.

Cracked glass.

What the…?

The memory of her SUV shuddering beneath her…the odd up-and-down motion that felt as if she'd been driving over a bumpy road when she hadn't even started the engine…zoomed into her head with a sensory detonation that made her groan even louder. She'd gotten into the vehicle after her visit to her tax accountant's office. She remembered closing the door. And then the sudden vibrations…

The distinct whine of metal made her breath catch.

Lisa's gaze jerked upward.

It took a full five seconds for her brain to absorb and comprehend what her eyes saw.

The roof of her SUV was dented…jutting downward…only inches from her head.

How was that possible?

Her vision blurred and she squeezed her eyes shut to slow the spinning inside her head.

Pull it together, she ordered her mind, which instantly tried to go fuzzy on her again.

Had she been in an accident?

Earthquake. The word surfaced through her confusion, and she knew without further examination that one had occurred. That's why she'd felt the vehicle moving even before she started the engine.

But she was safe…inside the parking garage.

Something that sounded like an explosion rent the air. The SUV creaked and groaned, the sounds nearly deafening.

"Think, Lisa," she muttered. "Pull it together." She sat up a little straighter, careful not to bump her head against the roof of the vehicle. Taking a deep breath for good measure, she focused on her surroundings.

Her heart rushed into her throat when she realized that the garage had collapsed around her. She could barely see between the piles of rubble. She couldn't make out any other vehicles. But there had to be others. She remembered clearly noting several cars when she'd emerged from the stairwell onto the third level.

The response was automatic. A woman, whether it was daylight or dark, never entered a parking garage without taking stock of her surroundings. It was just common sense.

The pounding in her chest brought her attention back to the immediate problem. How to get out…

She tried the driver's door. Grunting, she pushed with all her might. The door didn't budge. She didn't even bother with the passenger side. A huge concrete pillar had blocked that side of the vehicle. She shivered. A few more inches to the left and it would have completely crushed her car.

"Think!" She had to get out of here. Chunks of broken concrete had smashed the car's hood inward. No doubt the engine was damaged beyond repair. The windshield had cracked. She surveyed the roof of the SUV again. It had caved inward, which meant there had to be more rubble on top. She felt certain that every second she remained in the vehicle put her in more danger.

The weary echo of the fatigued structure that had only hours ago been a four-story parking garage punctuated the thought. She had no doubt that whatever remained intact would soon collapse completely. She had to get out!

Ignoring the throb in her skull, she scrambled over the seat and tried the door behind the driver's. It opened, but only a few inches. Not far enough for her to squeeze out.

"Damn it!"

The power windows wouldn't work. No surprise there, considering the condition of the hood.

The rear hatch.

Clambering over the seat and into the cargo compartment, she shoved against the hatch door. No luck.

Panic slid through her, making it nearly impossible to think clearly. She had to concentrate!

She kicked at the window in the hatch. It opened

separately from the door. That might be her only chance of escape. The latch was on the outside. From what she could tell in the dim lighting, there was enough space for the window part to lift up. All she had to do was get it open. She kicked at it again. It didn't budge.

She needed something to break the glass.

Lisa tamped down the rising panic and fumbled with the carpet beneath her feet. The spare-tire compartment would have a jack. She could use that. Her fingers felt numb and wouldn't work properly.

"Hurry…hurry," she urged, knowing that she was quickly losing the battle with her fear.

A sound like thunder rumbling in over the ocean jerked her attention upward. The whole parking garage shuddered.

She had to get out of here.

She needed help.

Her cell phone.

Lisa scrambled back to the front seat and found her purse. By the time she found her phone, her fingers were trembling and her throat had gone so dry she wasn't sure speech would be possible. She had to let someone know she was in here before she did anything else.

Closing her eyes, she held the phone a moment and took a deep, halting breath. She had to calm down. Time was running out; she had to make herself clear. She couldn't screw up what might be her last chance at rescue.

Focusing on the small keys, she entered the three most significant numbers known to any American alive.

911.

A new knot of panic tightened in her throat as ring after ring shrilled in her ear.

Why wasn't the operator answering?

Was the whole city damaged so badly that even emergency services were out of commission?

Dear God, she hadn't thought of that.

What about her family…the clinic?

The animals?

Greg?

What about…*Joe?*

He would be in the middle of the devastation, attempting to rescue victims like her.

"911. What is the nature of your emergency?"

Tears stung Lisa's eyes.

"I'm trapped," she managed to say past the lump in her throat. "I need help."

"Give me your location, ma'am," the operator said with amazing calm.

"I'm…I'm…" For just one moment her mind went blank. Lisa clamped down on her lower lip and stemmed the tears that tried to flow. Calm. She had to be calm. "I'm in the parking garage." She gave the address.

"Yes, ma'am. We already have a rescue team there. Can you tell me which level you parked on when you entered the garage?"

"I parked on the…" Another moment of uncertainty. "The third level," she said quickly. "The rubble is all around my car. I can't get out. It…" More creaking and groaning tugged at her attention. "It sounds like the whole thing is going to collapse. Please." She couldn't hold back the emotion from her voice this time. *"Help me."*

CHAPTER TWO

"CAP'N!"

Joe turned as Spike double-timed it over to his position. "What's up?" If this was another attempt to talk him out of going in again, Spike might as well save his breath. Every instinct warned Joe that there were more victims trapped. *Victims still breathing.* He had to do all he could to see that everyone got out safely.

It was more than just his job…it was the right thing to do.

"Dispatch's got a vic on the horn," Spike explained. "She called in on her cell phone. Says she's trapped on level three, far side." His gaze focused solemnly on Joe's. "There's rubble all around her vehicle, a gray SUV. The power windows have been disabled and she hasn't been able to kick her way out."

Damn. Joe shook his head. Women should always carry a brick in their cars for that reason. If the power windows failed, they could break the glass.

"All right," he told Spike. "That's where I'm headed."

"Cap'n." O'Shea pushed her way into the discussion. "Going back in there now would be suicide."

Leave it to O'Shea to state the obvious so plainly. "And if I don't, the lady dies," he countered.

His loyal firefighter glanced away. "I know." Her gaze swung back to his, renewed determination there. "Then we'll both go in. You'll need backup."

He was shaking his head before the answer had time to form on his tongue. "No way. I'm not taking anyone in there with me." Quickly he checked his gear. Getting back out might not be easy. With O'Shea shadowing his step, he headed back to the truck for a rappelling rope. "Get a canine over here and find out how soon we can have some heavy equipment on-site. Just in case," he added over his shoulder as he checked his communications mike.

A few other members of his squad had gathered around him by then. All knew exactly what his last comment meant. The heavy equipment was in case he didn't make it out and they had to start searching for bodies, including his own, rather than survivors. Backhoes and the like were the least desirable method for uncovering survivors.

"I think we should check with the ICS commander before we—" Spike began.

"In case you haven't noticed," Joe challenged, "we're in the middle of a crisis here. There's a lot more damage than just this parking garage. Those in charge have their hands full. We'll do this my way. The situation is far too unstable to risk any more lives than absolutely necessary. No one follows me in unless I call for help. No one." He looked from O'Shea to the others, making eye contact with each one, leaving nothing to speculation. "Is that understood?"

A rumble of reluctant *Yes, Cap'n*'s went through the group.

"All right. Get dispatch to patch into my com link. I need direct contact with the lady if I'm going to find her."

"Yes, sir."

The members of Joe's squad dispersed. Some left to task work with the engineers, surveying the damage to check for possible passages in which to search for trapped victims once a canine unit was on-site. Others would help tend injuries and route patients to the hospital as necessary. But Joe knew that every single member of his team would be on high alert, fully prepared to come in after him if need be.

He surveyed the garage once more.

The stairwell and elevator shaft leading to the upper levels were damaged beyond use, even if he'd been inclined to take the risk. Not much remained in the way of structural support. Joe had a bad feeling that the entire garage could go anytime now. Whoever this lady was, she was definitely living on borrowed time. He hoped like hell he could get to her in time.

The climb around and over massive piles of concrete and twisted metal took longer this time. There was no easy access to what remained of the third deck.

Joe paused to swipe the grimy sweat from his forehead. "Any luck on that patch?" he asked, knowing his question would be carried via his communications link to his squad. He needed more specific directions. The garage was pretty damn big and could accommodate a number of cars. The "far side" didn't narrow things down much.

"Working on it, Cap'n," came O'Shea's voice.

He had to move with extreme caution now. The slightest shift in weight could cause a concrete avalanche. He let out an uneasy breath when he visually assessed the extent of the damage on level three. Getting to the opposite side wouldn't be a simple thing.

Clenching his jaw, he started the perilous journey. His gaze narrowed as he scanned the piles of broken concrete and twisted iron for any sign of the SUV. The victim had said it was gray. Thank God for cell phones. If he was able to get her out, she would owe her life to that sometimes annoying device.

He reached for a piece of protruding rebar to pull himself up. The rubble shifted. Joe froze, not daring to breathe. A low growl filled the air half a second before the pile of rocks beneath him shuddered then dropped a good three feet. Joe held on to the support as best he could.

The grinding sound of concrete and steel was almost deafening as the rubble settled once more, flinging Joe forward. He struggled to regain his footing.

"Cap'n, you there?"

The worried voice echoed in Joe's ear. "I'm here. Level three is in bad shape. I'm attempting to make my way across to the other side."

"Stand by for the patch," O'Shea said. "I've been giving dispatch down the road for taking their sweet time."

"Standing by." Joe reached up for a better handhold

in the rock pile. One step forward, two back. The knot in his gut tightened a little more, reminding him that this was not good. He told himself he'd been in dire straits before. This wasn't the first time he'd put his life on the line to save a vic.

But things were different now.

He frowned. Where the hell had that thought come from? Nothing in his life had changed. He still enjoyed being single, loved the hell out of his work. His life was perfect. He had no one to answer to except himself. No strings, no hassles.

An image of Lisa Malloy suddenly loomed large inside his head. Now, why the hell would he think of her at a time like this?

He swallowed hard and tried to focus on the goal, moving across this treacherous rock pile that had once been the third floor of the parking garage.

She'd changed something inside him. There was no denying that, no matter how hard he tried. She'd gotten to him in a way that no one ever had. He couldn't figure it out. She was cute as hell, that was true. Had a great personality and was as dedicated to her work as he was to his, which gave them something in common.

But that's where the common ground ended. She had marriage and kids on her mind—something Joe had no interest in whatsoever. Not that he didn't expect to marry at some point in his life. But not right now. After all, he was only thirty-three. It wasn't as if time was running out.

Just then his foot slipped and it took all his strength

to prevent himself from falling. Joe glanced down at the jagged slope that dropped all the way to the lowest level. Ugly. And there was no way to determine where the rubble was stable and where it wasn't. Falling or ending up being buried alive were two very real possibilities in a situation like this.

Maybe time was a little shorter than he'd thought.

This was definitely no time for distractions.

Not even desirable ones like Lisa.

His body instantly hardened at the memory of the last time they had made love. She got to him so easily, made him weak...made him need her. She was the first and only woman who had ever made him think beyond the moment...beyond the physical aspect of the relationship.

He almost laughed at himself. Relationships? He didn't do relationships. Not Joe Ripani. Even the definition of *relationship* was too definite for him.

And yet, on some level, his and Lisa's time together had felt exactly like that. Definite.

Though they'd parted ways a full three weeks ago, a twinge of something like hurt sliced through him even now. It was crazy. He shouldn't be thinking of her anymore. He should have moved on without a second thought.

But no matter how hard he tried, he would wake up in the middle of the night with images of her haunting his dreams. With the taste of her lingering on his lips, and the need for her touch a palpable longing in his loins.

His heart constricted in his chest. He hoped like hell she was safe at the clinic. If she'd been trapped at home or on the street somewhere, she would worry herself silly over those animals. He'd never known a more dedicated veterinarian. He thought of Salvage and realized that it was that damn dog that had thrown him and Lisa together. O'Shea had rescued the injured mutt from a burning building, but Joe was the one who'd taken over routine care after the animal became the firehouse mascot—not that he minded. That's what had put him in regular contact with Lisa.

If it hadn't been for Salvage, Joe might never have ended up with his heart turning traitor against him. He was fully accustomed to waltzing on the edge of survival in his line of work, but this dancing on the fringes of emotional commitment was foreign to him.

What would a guy like him do with a wife and family? Later, when he was chief or something, it would be okay. But what kind of life could he offer a woman right now? He dived into dangerous situations for a living. It wouldn't be fair to any woman, and certainly not to children. He didn't want to leave a wife and kids behind if he suffered an untimely death. And unfortunately, that possibility came with the territory in his occupation.

Like now, a little voice taunted.

Adrenaline burned through him as his boot sent pebbles clattering down the slope. Nope, this was definitely not the kind of job for a man with a family. He was better off staying unattached.

No matter how much he would love to make Lisa a permanent part of his off-duty routine, it would never work. No-strings-attached sex was not her style. She would never be satisfied with an uncommitted relationship. He knew it. She knew it. Enough said.

The moment she'd asked that dreaded question, he'd known it was over. Those seven seemingly innocuous words had filled his usually brave heart with dread.

Where do you see our relationship going?

Wedding bells had clanged in his head, and dread had pooled in his gut. He'd had to break it off then and there. She'd been hurt, but it was far less painful than it would have been had they pursued the kind of relationship she wanted.

He'd done the right thing.

He hoped again that she was safe at home or at the clinic. Though he might not want to make anything permanent with her, he still cared…a lot.

"Cap'n."

O'Shea. Joe hesitated, something in the tone of her voice giving him pause. "I'm here. Got that patch for me?" He needed to be speaking directly with the victim—needed any details she could give him to direct him to her position.

"I got it, Cap'n, but there's something you should know before I put her through." O'Shea's voice trembled on the last words.

"Time's wasting, O'Shea."

A beat of silence passed before she said two words that would impact Joe as nothing else could. "It's Lisa."

A moment of pure panic slammed into his brain. "Lisa Malloy?" he demanded, as if there was any other Lisa in his life or O'Shea's.

"She says it's bad, Cap'n. Real bad. I'm patching her through now."

"Joe?"

Joe's heart stumbled at the sound of Lisa's voice. He blinked rapidly. At the dust, he told himself. "Yeah, I'm here," he said with as much nonchalance as he could muster. "Tell me where you're at so I can come rescue you."

"I'm...I'm on the side of the garage opposite the Welton Building."

At least he was headed in the right direction. The Welton Building, which housed a number of offices, was at his back.

"Be a little more specific if you can," he prodded gently. He'd heard the fear in her voice. Fear, hell. She had to be scared to death. His gaze searched frantically for any sign of her car. He should have known when he'd heard gray SUV. Lisa drove an SUV and it was what he'd call silver. Somewhere in the back of his mind he'd acknowledged the possibility. But denial was a strong ally at times.

"I parked in the middle...you know, not all the way at the end, but not very close to the stairwell, either. I...I don't know. Is that specific enough?"

"Sure...I'll be right there," he lied for her benefit. He couldn't see a damn thing. Nothing but monochromatic heaps of rubble.

"It's bad, Joe," she murmured so softly he scarcely heard her.

"I've seen worse." Another flat-out lie, he thought,

moving as quickly as he dared. "Tell me what you see out your windows."

His heart pounded so hard during the silence that followed that his head filled with the roar of blood rushing there, pushing against his eardrums.

"Piles of broken concrete," she said, her voice not shaking quite so badly now. "There's a support pillar lying against the hood of my car. Maybe another one on top, since the roof over the front seat is bashed in."

A new surge of fear hit like a fist to his already tense gut. "You got plenty of room to move around in there?" he asked carefully, not wanting to give away how much that part concerned him.

"Yes…sort of. I moved to the cargo area in hopes of getting out through the rear hatch, but I didn't have any luck kicking out the glass."

"Is the hatch clear of debris?" That would be a stroke of fiercely needed luck.

"Partially."

"Good. That's the way we'll get you out then." He made the statement as if it were a given, but the farther he moved into this level, the dimmer that prospect looked.

The structure still moaned, and Joe knew there was a real risk of total collapse. Time was running out.

"Lisa, do me a favor, would you?" He had to pinpoint her location. Now.

"Be careful, Ripani," she said softly, almost laughingly. "The last time I did you a favor, it turned out badly."

She was remembering Salvage's injuries…the way she'd healed the animal that was now part of the fire-house team. No, it wasn't Salvage or his injuries on her mind. She was likely recalling his callousness, his ability to walk away as if nothing had happened between them. She didn't have to say it; he understood. And he had walked away, just like that. The decision had been mutual once he'd made his position clear. He'd had his reasons. But he knew she hadn't understood, though she'd claimed to. He wasn't even sure he could explain it. Now definitely wasn't the time to try.

"No strings attached, babe," he teased, infusing the words with a chuckle. "Try the horn or radio." He doubted the radio worked since the power windows didn't, but it was worth a shot. And though it could be dangerous to sound a horn in such an unstable structure, Joe had to take the risk. "I need to know exactly where you are."

"Okay."

He held his position while he waited for her to attempt to signal him. He sweated out every single second before the sound of the horn cut through the silence. "Once more," he told her. He homed in on the direction of the sound. "Gotcha."

"Hurry, Joe," she urged, the fear back in her voice now. "I don't know how much longer the roof is going to hold out."

Did that mean the weight of the rubble was pressing in on her? Joe swore under his breath and moved faster. He had to get her out of there. Every instinct warned him that total collapse was imminent.

"Give us a status, Cap'n."

O'Shea's voice cut into his thoughts. Her connection would override the patch with Lisa.

"Stay off the link," he growled. He wanted nothing between him and Lisa.

"We need a status on your situation," she repeated. "I've got a canine standing by. Do you need backup?"

O'Shea was prepared to come in. Joe imagined it had more to do with saving her best friend than with supporting her captain, but he'd give her that. He wanted to save Lisa, as well. Though Shannon O'Shea was professional to the bone, even the best-trained rescue workers couldn't completely set aside emotion when someone close was in danger.

"Stand down, O'Shea," he ordered. "I've got the situation under control. Now clear the link."

"Yes, sir."

"Joe, are you still there?"

Lisa's voice. He wondered now why he'd never noticed how pleasant it was. It touched him as gently as a butterfly's wing and with a sweetness that took his breath. How could any man have known this woman intimately and not be affected, even if he had walked away?

How could a guy walk away from a woman like Lisa?

What was wrong with him? What idiot would pass on a future with a woman like her? O'Shea had pointed that out to him the day after he'd split with Lisa. Up until then, Shannon had never once given him any grief on the job. And then only that one time. She'd said her piece and hadn't spoken of it since. Still, he knew she was disappointed in him where Lisa was concerned. O'Shea carefully kept her feelings out of their professional relationship, but Joe knew where she stood on the issue of Lisa. And like Lisa, O'Shea just didn't understand that he'd done the only thing he could.

He had those old reliable reasons for the decision he'd made. The ones that had kept him single when his friends, as well as his squad members, had gotten married one by one. But he knew what was right for him. A permanent relationship had no place in his life.

Any fool could see that.

He just couldn't figure why it felt so damn wrong right now.

Truth be told, it had felt wrong way before now. He'd missed Lisa. Thought about her more than he would admit even to himself. Wanted her desperately.

But having her would be…a mistake.

He'd told himself that three weeks ago.

Jesus, he prayed, don't let this be the Almighty's way of showing him what a mistake he'd made.

"Joe?"

The desperate plea in her voice tugged hard on Joe's heartstrings. Strings he hadn't realized he possessed. But then, he'd realized a lot of things in the past four or five minutes.

"I'm almost there," he assured her.

"Joe, I want you to know that—"

"You don't have to say anything," he said, cutting her off. He wasn't sure he could deal with true confessions right now. Good, bad or indifferent.

"You always were a stubborn male chauvinist pig," she snapped.

His eyebrows shot upward. "I guess I can't deny that," he allowed humbly. At least if she was pissed at him she wouldn't have time to focus on her fear.

"Deny it?" she said hotly. "Please. The only person you ever think of in a relationship is you. You just pretend no one counts except you, then when you walk away, it doesn't ping your conscience because you've convinced yourself you didn't do anything wrong or hurt anyone."

"Okay," he relented. "I was wrong. I shouldn't have slept with you then walked away."

He could almost see her stewing on the other end of the communications link. Without a word, she telegraphed her fury with a quiet that thickened between them.

"That's all it was to you, wasn't it?" she said. "Plain old physical gratification. Not making love, just sex."

His frown deepened. Maybe he did deserve a good tongue-lashing, but she'd enjoyed the sex just as much as he had. To pretend otherwise was a flat-out denial of the truth.

"We were both over twenty-one, honey," he retorted, his own irritation surfacing now. "It's not like I talked you into anything you didn't want to do."

The silence was different this time, and he muttered a self-deprecating curse. Talk about inserting foot in mouth. Good thing they were on this line alone.

"Look, I shouldn't have said that. Let's just focus here." He glanced around at the destruction and then shook himself. What the hell was he doing, letting his attention stray? Only Lisa had ever been able to do that to him.

She sighed. "Sorry. You're right. Just get me out of here, please."

"Almost there." He zeroed in on the spot where he'd determined her SUV to be. A grin slid across his face. He could see the rear hatch. "Gotcha in my sights, babe."

"Thank God."

Ditto, he mused.

They would talk about this later. When they were both safe. And when the city was back to normal again. When he finished up here, chances were there would be other missions related to Mother Nature's handiwork waiting for him.

Getting Lisa to safety was about all he and his squad could accomplish at this site. The canines and heavy equipment would have to take it from here.

Lisa gasped. "I see you!"

He smiled for her benefit, though he couldn't quite make her out just yet. The lightly tinted rear window prevented him from seeing inside the vehicle, but he was almost there.

The entire structure suddenly shook.

Not just a slight shift.

Not a mere reaction to mounting stress on the compromised support beams.

Aftershock.

Joe bit back a heated curse and pushed forward.

He had to get to Lisa.

The rubble beneath him shifted.

A loud boom thundered above him. Debris fell around him, the low-pitched roar sounding like the enthusiastic clapping of hands.

Joe curled into a ball and shielded his head.

Chunks of glass and concrete rained down on him, followed by clouds of dust.

The shaking stopped as suddenly as it had started, and an eerie quiet fell.

Lisa.

Freeing himself from the rubble, he strained to see her car.

A distant rumble drew his gaze upward in time to see another section of the upper level falling.

He scrambled for cover but he couldn't get a footing.

Then it was silent again…

…and dark.

CHAPTER THREE

LISA CURLED into the smallest ball possible and wrapped her arms over her head as she hunkered in the cargo compartment of the SUV.

The whole world seemed to tremble with fear.

Was this it?

The end?

Dear God, what about Joe?

She unfurled herself even before the vehicle stopped groaning beneath the weight of more rubble.

She had to know if he was all right.

Had to see.

To get out.

She couldn't help him from in here.

"Joe!"

The silence that reverberated across the airwaves and into her ear sent her heart plummeting to her feet.

"Joe! Please, answer me! Joe, are you all right?"

"Lisa!"

Shannon's voice.

"Lisa, where's Joe?" Her voice warbled slightly.

Lisa's pulse throbbed in her brain. It had to be bad if

Shannon was worried. She was always so strong. Please, please, God, don't let Joe be dying out there.

"Lisa, we've lost contact with Joe. Are you all right?"

"I can't see him," she murmured, her own voice stumbling. "I can't—"

"Lisa, listen to me," Shannon commanded. "Are you all right?"

She tried to calm down, forcing herself to look around the car and size up the situation. Okay. She was okay.

Just then a vicious creak split the air and the roof buckled in, pressing down on her.

Glass shattered.

"The roof is caving in," Lisa cried. She edged closer to the rear hatch. The middle of the SUV was crushed so far down that the interior ceiling light was now flattened against the console.

She couldn't move.

Couldn't breathe.

She was going to die.

"Lisa, I heard glass shattering. Are you still with me?"

She nodded mutely, then struggled to respond audibly. "Yes." She couldn't move...could scarcely breathe.

Joe. God, where was Joe?

"Can you climb out? Maybe through one of the windows?"

Lisa started shaking her head before her friend completed the question. All the windows were shattered, flattened into triangular slits only a few inches high.

No way could she get out.

"I can't..."

She tried to see behind her. Where was Joe?

"Joe!" she shouted. *Please, please, don't let him be dead.* "Joe! Can you hear me?"

"Lisa, stay with me," Shannon urged. "Is the window in the rear hatch still intact?"

Lisa turned her head as best she could. "Yes."

"Can you maneuver around and kick it out?"

"I tried that already." Her heart had leaped into her throat. "I couldn't do it. I…I can't turn around. I'm stuck."

"Try, Lisa! You've got to try. You might be able to kick out the glass now with the added pressure."

"Where's Joe?" Lisa repeated, tears stinging her eyes. She tried to see but the car seemed buried in rubble. There was still some dim light coming through the hatch, which gave her hope, but what about Joe? She stretched, tried to move.

Turn around. She had to turn around. Something sharp jabbed her shoulder. She winced but kept working at freeing herself.

"Bull's trying to get him now. Let's concentrate on getting you out of that vehicle."

Shannon said something to one of the others…

"No!" Lisa shouted. "Don't you try to come in here, Shannon. It's too late. Just…" There was no way anyone could get to her. Defeat twisted like barbwire in her stomach. She was certain of it now. Joe was likely dead and soon she would be, too.

She squeezed her eyes shut and tried to hold back the tears. Damn it. Who would take care of her animals? What about her family? They would be devastated.

And what about Joe?

The tears flowed now as she remembered the last time she'd seen him. He'd dropped by the clinic to break a date with her. She had to give him that. He had been man enough to let her down in person.

She had pretended indifference. As if it didn't matter either way. But she'd known what had sent him running.

Where do you see our relationship going?

She'd asked the impossible of him.

Joe Ripani just wasn't the marrying kind.

It certainly didn't matter now.

Nothing mattered now…

"Lisa?"

Her breath caught.

"I'm here, babe."

Joe.

The sound of his voice sent her heart into a frantic rhythm.

He was alive.

"Joe!" She bit down on her lower lip to stem the new rush of tears. "You scared the hell out of me, Ripani."

"Scared myself," he admitted with a chuckle. "Had to dig my way back to the surface."

Fear stabbed deep into her chest. "Are you all right?" She could imagine broken bones and hemorrhaging. Men never liked to admit when they were injured. He probably needed medical attention. The dead last thing he should do was crawl deeper into this hellhole.

"'Course I'm all right. You think a little something like a few thousand pounds of concrete is going to stop me?"

This wasn't the time for jokes. He could save that iceman persona for someone who didn't know him better.

"Joe, I—"

The whole structure shook again. The metal SUV screeched beneath the weight bearing down on it.

Dear God, this whole place was going to collapse.

"You should get out of here, Joe," she said. Her voice had gone flat, emotionless. It was over. No point in both of them ending up dead. "Don't come any closer. You'll never be able to get me out."

"I'm almost there."

She shook her head. "No. Don't do this." She managed to squeeze to one side as the hatch was compressed even further. She was trapped completely now. Couldn't even turn her head.

"Just go," she urged him. "The whole place is going to fall in. You can't get me out of here. The car is squashed down around me."

Defeat sucked the oxygen right out of her lungs.

Shannon. "Shannon said she was coming in, too," Lisa blurted. "You have to stop her, Joe. Go back. Don't let anyone else come in here. Please don't play the hero. It's…" She took stock of the situation again and surrendered to the inevitable. "It's too late."

Something bumped against the glass behind her. She couldn't turn around.

"It's me," he said, only this time his voice came through the glass instead of over her cell phone.

She wanted to turn around…to see him one last time

and tell him how sorry she was that things hadn't worked out between them…but she couldn't move.

"Can you slide down just a little? Get beneath the glass."

The urgency in his voice prodded at her. It was too late. Why didn't he just go? Why risk his life, as well? Because that's what he did, she answered herself. That's who he was.

Joe Ripani was a real hero. He liked the part, no matter the risk. It was who he was.

"I'll try." She slid downward, forcing her body against the damaged metal and tattered headliner that had once been the roof of her SUV. Sharp edges snagged her blouse, scraping at her skin, but she kept squirming to do as Joe asked.

"Close your eyes and protect your face if you can."

She released her cell phone and shielded her face with the one hand she could move.

He pried at the window…she could hear him grunting with the effort.

The glass shattered.

Suddenly his hands were pulling at her.

With the glass gone, she squeezed out through the opening as he tucked the crowbar he'd been using into his gear belt.

And then she was in his arms.

The tears flowed like a river. She couldn't have stopped them if she'd bothered trying.

He was okay.

He was really okay.

His arms felt so strong around her.

"We have to get out of here," he murmured softly against her ear. "The whole place is going to cave in."

She nodded and reluctantly drew back from his embrace.

Damn, he looked good.

She wanted to stare at him, to take in every last detail of that handsome face. But they had to move.

He clambered over and around the heaps of rubble, dragging her behind him.

Barely recognizable parts of vehicles pierced through the mounds of fallen concrete and steel but Lisa kept her gaze steady on Joe. If she stopped to look—to think— she'd lose it. She had to keep moving. For both their sakes.

Another rumble…another vibration.

"Aftershocks?" she asked.

"Probably the underlying structure…it's going to give way completely," he said.

She remembered thinking that only moments ago. Her heart hammered viciously. What if they couldn't get out after all?

Joe swore. The heat of it seared through her.

They were trapped.

The path they'd followed was now fully blocked by the collapse of the level above.

"We'll have to try another egress route," he suggested as he started in a different direction.

Joe spoke quietly via his communications link to his team, who were standing by to assist in any way possible. But there was nothing they could do.

It was all up to him now.

An odd kind of calm settled over Lisa. Joe knew what he was doing. If anyone could get them out of here, he could.

He pulled her after him, weaving over and between slabs of concrete. The place looked like a war zone. The destruction was unbelievable…overwhelming. She prayed again that no one had died in what must be dozens of crushed automobiles.

"Things are going to get a little tricky here," he said as he came to a stop.

Lisa tried to focus, but her cognitive processes were pretty much on automatic now.

"We've got to snake our way through here to get to the other side."

She considered the mountain of broken construction material before them. No way over it or around it. That much was true. Then she stared at the narrow, tunnel-like hole he indicated.

This void went down…under the debris.

That could be a death sentence.

"I can't…" She shook her head to emphasize her words. No way could she crawl into that hole.

He took her by the shoulders and gave her a gentle shake. "It's the only way, babe. It might be nothing but a dead end, but we can't just stand here and wait for the inevitable. I'll go first."

For three beats she could only stare into those dark eyes. His face was dusty and grimy, as were his clothes. He looked nothing like the spit-and-polish, suave guy who had a reputation with the ladies. She had a sudden, nearly overwhelming urge to laugh. Hysteria. She knew the symptoms. As funny and out of character as he looked, he was dead serious.

She forced her head in an up-and-down motion. "Okay."

He knew what he was doing. This wasn't her area of expertise. If he thought they needed to crawl under the rocks, then by God, she'd follow him into that hole.

He was, after all, that kind of hero.

Again, she had to stifle the urge to laugh. Hysteria had taken root. Focus, she ordered her dizzy brain. She had to do just what he told her…she had to keep it together. Had to listen carefully to his instructions.

JOE SQUEEZED through the opening to the tunnel, tilting his shoulders at odd angles to manage the feat. Lisa stayed right behind him. She was scared. The fear in those blue eyes had been palpable. He'd wanted to hold her and tell her everything would be all right, but there was no time for that. Every second they stayed in this garage pushed them closer to the edge of no return.

If this passage turned out to be a dead end…well, he'd just deal with it.

He stalled at the next turn. Damn, the pathway narrowed here. Maybe he should have let Lisa go first. She was tiny enough to slip through without much effort. He still couldn't be sure that this would take them where they needed to go. But he was banking on the light. The tunnel would be pitch-dark if the other end was closed.

The dim light gave him hope. He prayed it would be enough.

Grunting with the brutal effort it took, Joe twisted sideways and forced his big body through the passageway. Thankfully, the end of the tunnel seemed just beyond this turn. The light was much brighter there. Good sign.

They'd almost made it.

Thank God.

He almost shouted with relief when he reached the narrow exit. A short scramble over the rocks and they'd be out of this hole.

"Give me your hand." He reached for Lisa, and the two of them climbed up and out of the makeshift passage. "You okay?"

She nodded stiffly. Her clothes were covered in dust, but he saw no sign of injury. No blood.

They were close now.

The location of the stairwell and elevator shaft was only a few feet away. They wouldn't be able to use either of those routes, of course, but he'd figure out something. The knots of tension in his gut tightened, ratcheting up his anxiety. They had to get out of here. Right now. Every instinct was screaming a warning at him.

Joe zigzagged his way through the fallen rubble until he reached the far half wall on the outside of the garage. Relief surged through him as he stared down into a narrow opening next to where the stairwell had once stood. He could actually see all the way to the ground below.

He reached over his shoulder and retrieved his rappelling line. "Spike, O'Shea, you still with me?"

O'Shea's relieved voice came across the communications link. He quickly related their approximate location and the intended egress. The team would assemble on the ground below in case he needed assistance. Getting Lisa out of here was top priority.

He eased back from the wall and turned to her. She looked terrified. "I'm going to lower you down to Shannon." Maybe it would comfort Lisa to know her friend waited below. He glanced back outside and saw that O'Shea, along with four others, were ready and waiting to assist.

"What about you?"

The uncertainty that glittered in her eyes almost undid him. Why did she care? He knew he'd hurt her when he'd backed off their...*relationship*. And yet she still cared what happened to him.

Basic human compassion, he told himself.

Nothing more. She'd likely gotten over him already. She took in stray dogs and cats all the time with every bit as much compassion. Her concern for him was nothing outside the norm for Lisa Malloy. Nothing he wouldn't expect...and yet it touched him somehow.

"I'll climb down as soon as you're on the ground," he explained.

She blinked rapidly, a frown drawing her sweet face into a scowl. "But how will you—"

He snaked the line around her waist. "Don't worry about me, babe. I know what I'm doing." He gave her a few quick instructions on how to pull the line down around her hips and then how to hold on so she didn't slip. She paid close attention though he sensed that his every touch disturbed her almost as much as their current predicament. He imagined that she didn't feel comfortable being touched by him since he'd walked away so easily from what they'd shared.

If she only knew.

Easy had not been the way of it.

She stepped into the narrow opening that would take her to freedom as he tugged on his gloves.

"Now, swing your legs over the edge of the wall and I'll lower you down," he said as casually as if she did this sort of thing every day.

Her gaze locked with his. "You…you won't drop me?"

It took all his strength not to kiss the hell out of her. That pouty bottom lip trembled, tempting him almost beyond endurance.

"Not a chance."

She nodded, then did as he'd instructed.

He heard her gasp as she dropped free of the shelf the remaining wall formed, but he had her. Slowly, but surely, he lowered her through the narrow crevasse to safety. Cheers went up as O'Shea tugged the line free from Lisa and gave Joe a nod. As he hoisted up the line, he watched the two women embrace and couldn't help feeling a little jealous that it wasn't him holding Lisa like that.

"Idiot," he muttered. He'd had his chance. He'd walked away. He couldn't go down that road with her or anyone else. Staying single was the right thing to do. No matter how wrong it felt at the moment.

LISA WATCHED as Joe rappelled downward as easily as he would walk across a room. When his feet touched the ground, the whole squad flocked to him, thankful their leader had survived.

As she stared up at the collapsed parking garage that she had used so many times, Lisa swallowed hard. It just didn't seem possible that a building could crumble like that. As if it were made of sand and fragile sticks rather than concrete and steel. But it had.

She closed her eyes and thanked God yet again that she and Joe had made it out safely. It was an absolute miracle that neither of them had been killed.

A wave of dizziness washed over her and she swayed on her feet.

Strong arms went immediately around her. "Whoa." Joe's deep, husky voice rumbled in her ear.

"I'm okay," she assured him as she pulled free of his embrace. "Really."

He didn't look convinced.

Shannon started to say something and Joe cut her a look. "Take it from here, O'Shea, I need to run Ms. Malloy by the hospital to be checked out."

Lisa looked from Joe to Shannon and back. "I'm fine."

Shannon seemed a little taken aback but didn't buck her captain's orders. "Yes, sir, Captain Ripani," she said sharply, and did an about-face without a word to Lisa.

Joe glared after her.

"I don't need to go to the hospital," Lisa said, drawing his attention back to her. "I'm fine. Really, Joe."

He studied her face and she suddenly felt embarrassed about how she must look. A mess, she felt certain.

What was wrong with her? She'd just survived an earthquake. Her car was a crushed metal pancake on what used to be the third level of that parking garage. She wasn't supposed to look good. And she owed her life to the guy who'd recently broken her heart.

"You're pretty shaken up, Lisa," he said in that soft, pleading tone that likely got him laid anytime he wanted.

Lisa tamped down a rush of jealousy. Her fling with Joe was over. She wasn't supposed to be jealous. Besides, he'd just saved her life. She should be grateful. She was! She just couldn't get past that other thing. The hurt.

"A little shocky, I'd guess," he went on, clearly oblivious to her mental tirade. "You need to be checked out and the paramedics here have their hands full." He shrugged those massive shoulders that would no doubt be bruised tomorrow from squeezing through that narrow passage. "Besides, you need a ride home anyway. We'd have to go right by the hospital to get to your place. Might as well stop by emergency just to be sure."

He had an answer for everything. And she was completely at his mercy.

That was the way with men like Joe Ripani. Women were putty in their hands.

Maybe he was right. Maybe she was a little shocky.

It might take her a few minutes, but one way or another, she promised herself, she would get her anti-Ripani defenses back into place. And when she did, he could just take his sweet-talking ways somewhere else. As much as she appreciated what he'd done for her, she couldn't risk letting herself fall into that trap again. Not if she hoped to survive.

She had his number and it added up to only one thing…heartbreak.

CHAPTER FOUR

THE UNEASY SILENCE in his truck unsettled Joe even more as he turned from Fifth Street onto Washington to head toward Courage Bay Hospital. He'd insisted that Lisa ride with him back to the firehouse where he could pick up his own truck. The search-and-rescue canines and heavy equipment had arrived at the parking garage just as Joe was leaving.

In an emergency like this, local jurisdiction resources would be somewhat overwhelmed with rescue and treatment. Assistance would be called in from surrounding communities. Joe and his squad had done the same many times. Just as soon as he was sure Lisa was good to go, he had every intention of getting back out in the field. This wasn't the sort of situation that would be resolved in a few hours. He let go a heavy breath. It would be a while before Courage Bay was back to normal. But the city was no stranger to disaster, and its emergency-services personnel had earned a reputation for excellence.

Lisa hadn't argued when he'd urged her toward his own vehicle. In fact, she hadn't said a word since they left the parking garage. At first he'd worried about shock, but he now had a feeling that she was simply annoyed at him.

She wasn't the kind of woman who cared for heroic tactics, and she would see his rescue of her as exactly that.

His fingers clenched the steering wheel. Funny thing, if he'd been trapped in that SUV, he would have been damn happy to have someone help him out. But not Lisa. No, she would consider any rescue attempt as the foolish act of an adrenaline junkie. She would rather have sacrificed herself than risk anyone else. That was something else they had in common, he realized abruptly.

Besides, he had to admit he'd been called far worse than an adrenaline junkie. The thing was, it usually didn't bother him. Somehow her rebuff did. He thought he'd gotten over his inability to impress a particular woman. Obviously that wasn't the case.

What was it about quiet, sensitive and highly intelligent Lisa Malloy that made him want to revert to adolescent tendencies?

He flicked a glance in her direction. Sure, she was pretty. Long, chestnut-colored hair that she wore up more often than not. Blue eyes the color of the Pacific when the sun hit the water just right. Her compact frame carried more visual punch than most petite women could possibly hope for. Lush curves and yet an athleticism that spoke of strength.

Damn. His entire body hardened. What was wrong with him? He didn't usually go gaga over any dame. Not this kind of gaga anyway. He didn't mind a serious case of lust—hell, he appreciated the hot, tingly feelings. The searing release that good, hot sex brought could only be called incredible. But this case of lust had stuck with him far longer than it should have. Lust was supposed to wear off after a few thorough sessions in the sack.

What the hell was the problem here?

He refused to consider the other four-letter word that tried to pop into his mind. The only *L* word he liked being acquainted with was l-u-s-t. Fast and furious and red-hot. That's the way he liked his short-term relationships, if he could call them relationships.

It was best for all concerned.

Plenty of physical pleasure without the emotional entanglements.

Lisa should be glad. He'd done her a favor.

Joe pulled into the emergency entrance of the hospital. As he'd anticipated, the place was buzzing with activity. He parked in the only remaining slot, which thankfully put them within a few feet of the entrance.

"This isn't necessary," Lisa insisted, breaking her long silence. "The doctors and nurses will be busy with real emergencies." She turned to him with a plea in those baby blues that twisted his gut all over again. "Just take me to the clinic. I need to check on the animals."

"I'm sure your pal Greg has everything under control." He made the statement with a little more sarcasm than he'd intended. There was something about Greg Seaborn that irked the hell out of Joe.

Climbing out of the truck, he hurried to the passenger side. Lisa didn't waste time arguing further. The man was completely hardheaded. She slid out when he opened her door, noting achy muscles for the first time. The little wave of dizziness had also set off a throbbing in her skull.

Maybe Joe was right. As he led the way through the chaos of the waiting area, she gently kneaded the right side of her head. She had herself a dandy lump. Made sense, now that she thought about it. She'd obviously been unconscious for a time after the earthquake hit. Considering the dizziness and the downright awful feeling in her stomach, a concussion was quite possible.

She wasn't sure how Joe managed the feat, but the next thing she knew, she was being hustled into a treatment room. The nurse promptly told Joe he would have to wait in the lobby.

"I'm afraid I can't do that," Joe said, smoothly countering the nurse's instructions, his charming voice as silky as ever. "You see, this patient is my responsibility."

Lisa resisted the urge to roll her eyes, especially considering that her entire skull was now pulsing on the verge of one hell of a headache.

The nurse looked from Joe to Lisa and back. "Well, in that case, you can wait in the corridor outside the room."

Joe smiled widely for the flustered nurse. "Yes, ma'am."

The smile he directed at Lisa before slipping out the door melted every ounce of irritation she'd managed to dredge up on the way here. How did he do that?

"You just relax, Ms. Malloy. The doctor will be in shortly." The nurse moved on to her next patient. How many others were there? Lisa didn't want to consider how many lives might be lost…how many injuries there were.

She reclined on the treatment table, thankful that she could lie still and close her eyes. She didn't want to think about the damage the earthquake had done to Courage Bay, or how many of the animals at her clinic had been injured. She didn't want to think at all right now.

As the nurse said, the doctor came in quickly and put her through a typical screening. He, too, worried there might be a mild concussion.

"Let's send you up to radiology," Dr. Winslow concluded. "Just to make sure there are no surprises."

Lisa tensed, chewing her lower lip. She couldn't ignore the possibility—not now. The risk was too great. "This may be a false alarm…" Her heart all but halted in her chest as she blurted in a near whisper, "There's a chance I could be pregnant."

For the space of two beats she held her breath, wanting desperately to snatch back the words. But there was no going back now. The idea that Joe stood right outside that door made her pulse skip.

The doctor smiled. "Let's get some blood work, then."

Lisa relaxed marginally. Okay. She would soon know. She needed to know. She'd put off finding out for too long.

Dr. Winslow moved on to other patients, and within moments of his departure, a lab tech arrived to take the necessary sample. To keep her mind off her own reality, she asked about other patients. According to the tech, the E.R. had been filled with people involved in automobile accidents related to the quake and others who'd been rescued from office buildings and homes. Lisa took some solace in the fact that there had been no fatalities reported as yet. She silently thanked God for looking out for Courage Bay's citizens.

The lab tech assured her that results would be back stat, but Lisa waited what passed like a lifetime for Dr. Winslow to return to the treatment room with the final word. Joe still waited in the corridor. Suddenly Lisa felt very tired. The nurse had popped back in with something for her headache. She had assured Lisa that it was safe to take the pain medication. Lisa understood what she meant. Safe, regardless of the test results.

Oh, God. If she was...

The clues had been there for the past two weeks. But Lisa felt certain she'd been in deep denial.

"Well, Ms. Malloy," Dr. Winslow said as the door closed behind him when he entered the treatment room at last, "I've got your results."

"Lisa," she insisted. Though she and Brad Winslow didn't know each other well, they'd met once or twice. His wife, Emily, had been thrilled when he'd brought her by the clinic to pick out a dog from among the ones Lisa had up for adoption. Every child needed a pet, and Emily and Brad wanted their baby to grow up with a dog.

He managed a half smile. "Lisa." A slight blush rose from his crisp white collar. "Based on your screening,

I'm certain there's a mild concussion, but unless your symptoms worsen, we'll forgo an X ray or scan for now. However, I would prefer that someone stay the night with you to monitor symptoms. If there is even the slightest change for the worse, I need you back here ASAP. I don't have to tell you that any kind of skull fracture is very serious business."

Lisa nodded. She knew very well what he meant.

He glanced down at her chart again before continuing. Dread coagulated in Lisa's veins.

Every instinct warned that he was about to give her news that would forever change her life.

At last he leveled his gaze on hers, and his neck reddened once more. "Ms. Malloy—"

"Lisa," she reminded.

"Sorry," he offered apologetically. "Lisa," he went on, "it's no false alarm. You are pregnant."

Though she'd known somewhere in the back of her mind that pregnancy was a distinct possibility when she'd missed her period three weeks ago, she'd somehow blocked the idea. Denial, no doubt. Deep, deep denial. She would still be in denial if she hadn't felt compelled to admit the possibility she was pregnant when faced with a routine screening for her head injury.

A dozen different emotions pelted her at once.

"I've been late before," she offered as an explanation for her earlier assertion that it might be a false alarm.

"How late are you?" he asked, one eyebrow slightly higher than the other.

She shrugged. "About three weeks."

"I see." He closed her chart. "Make an appointment to see an obstetrician. In the meantime, I'll be happy to prescribe some prenatal vitamins if you'd like."

Lisa tried to swallow, but her throat was too dry. "That would be fine. Thank you."

He searched her face. She knew what he was looking for—signs of what exactly she was feeling at the moment.

"You know, Lisa, having a child can be a real blessing." He smiled widely. "Trust me, I know." He sighed, his expression both wistful and dreamy. "You think you know how a child will change your life, but you don't." He gave his head a little shake. "There's no adequate way to describe just how wonderful fatherhood is."

She nodded awkwardly. Though she appreciated his attempt at making her feel comfortable with the news of her pregnancy, she just couldn't deal with it right now.

Obviously, he picked up on her discomfort.

"Well." He clasped her chart under his arm. "Someone will need to drive you home and I'll leave your release instructions at the desk." He made it a point not to mention Joe. Lisa was sure Brad knew Joe Ripani, since the firehouse was only blocks away, and Brad's brother, Cole, was a member of the K-9 patrol with Courage Bay's police department. She was immensely thankful Brad didn't query why the fireman who'd brought her to Emergency waited impatiently in the corridor rather than in the lobby.

"Thank you." She forced the words past her lips and managed to keep a smile in place until Brad was out the door. Once she was alone, her eyes closed and she fought to hold back the tears.

She was pregnant.

She'd always been so careful. How could she have messed up like this? And then the memory hit her.

Making love with Joe early in the morning…in the shower before they were both fully awake. Every other time they'd used a condom. They had only been careless that once.

All it takes is once, a little voice reminded.

She blinked back the sting of tears and ordered away the self-pity. She wanted children. Definitely. She just hadn't expected the child to come before the wedding.

But it happened. Quite frequently, she assured herself.

Oh, God…but not to her. What on earth was she going to do?

A kind of certainty clicked into place. "Get over it," she muttered. "That's all you can do."

It was done. She'd made a careless mistake and now she was pregnant. Some part of her was happy. She loved children. The baby would be beautiful, with Joe Ripani for a father. But she'd wanted so much for the children she'd planned to have. A good home, a loving father, a stable family network. Everything she'd had as a child.

That certainly wasn't going to happen. At least not all of it.

Ooooh. Her mother would never forgive her.

She shook off her gloom and slid from the table. Feeling sorry for herself wouldn't change a thing.

She was pregnant.

So what if it wasn't starting out the way she'd intended.

Having a baby was wonderful, wasn't it?

Brad had said so himself.

The urge to weep swept over her again.

Oh, God, what was she going to do?

Her parents would help—as soon as they got over the initial shock. Her sister. And she had friends. She could definitely depend on Shannon. But her child wouldn't have a father.

Agony twisted inside her, kicking aside the physical pain she'd been experiencing. She was pregnant. An unwed mother-to-be.

The consequences of that fact broadsided her next.

How could she let that happen?

Life was tough enough without starting off on the wrong foot. Single parents were a part of the norm now, especially with rising divorce rates, but she'd seen the downside. Fathers and mothers arguing over the best way to raise their kids…custody issues.

She had to do something. She did not want her child to have only one parent.

The realization that Joe was right outside the door abruptly knocked the breath out of her. She definitely couldn't deal with this right now.

She had to stay calm…had to keep a firm grip on her emotions. If he suspected for one second…

Don't go there, she ordered. Pull yourself together. Everything will be fine. Nothing to worry about.

She could fall apart when she got home…away from Joe.

She was pregnant.

SHE WAS PREGNANT.

Joe stood in the corridor outside the treatment room and felt the floor shift under his feet as if an aftershock had struck.

Lisa was pregnant.

He'd heard the doctor tell her, though he hadn't meant to eavesdrop.

He shoved his hands into his pockets. Okay, maybe he had. But when Brad Winslow reentered the room, Joe couldn't bear not to hear the news. He desperately needed to know if Lisa was all right. He'd been pacing out here for what felt like hours, worried she might have some sort of head injury that would require emergency surgery. Afraid she could be dying at that very moment.

But she was fine. He'd heard the doctor say so. Then he'd heard the shocking pronouncement.

You are pregnant.

Pregnant! She was going to have a baby.

She'd told the doctor that she was three weeks late. Joe might not be an expert on the workings of the female reproductive system, but he knew exactly what that meant. Lisa had gotten pregnant in the two or three weeks prior to when her period should have started.

He'd had a girlfriend once who'd used what she called the rhythm method of birth control. She'd assured him how safe it was, but Joe had insisted on the old reliable condom. He might like playing the field, but he also liked being responsible and safe.

He gave himself a mental shake and refocused on the issue here.

Lisa was pregnant. And the baby was his.

They had practiced safe sex…except that once.

Instantly the images of making love with Lisa in the shower bombarded his senses, hardened his already granitelike muscles. The taste of her…the sweet scent of her skin… He remembered it vividly. Making love to her that way had felt perfectly natural.

"Christ," he groaned.

He'd known something was up when Winslow came back with those test results. The guy had looked at Joe kind of funny. And then, when the doctor had left the treatment room, he'd avoided eye contact with Joe altogether. Admittedly, that part could have been Joe's imagination running away with him, but imagination or not, the pregnancy was real.

He was going to be a father. The weight of responsibility settled heavily onto his shoulders. He was only thirty-three. He hadn't expected to have children or a wife for some time yet.

But that time had come, whether he was ready or not.

He would not shirk his responsibilities. This was his baby and he intended to do right by the child.

A kind of numbness settled over him then. Damn…he

was going to be a father. He thought of all his pals at the firehouse, the married ones as well as the single. What would they think? They'd be shocked. Just the way he was.

No one ever put Joe Ripani in the same sentence with marriage, much less fatherhood.

Well, that was about to change.

Just then Lisa stepped out of the treatment room. His first thought was to announce to her that he knew about the baby and demand that they discuss exactly what they would do about it.

But then she'd know he'd been eavesdropping.

Not a good way to start off a permanent relationship. Even a commitment-avoiding guy like him knew the importance of trust in a relationship that was supposed to last a lifetime. Nope. He'd just have to wait for her to tell him. He'd have to pretend he didn't know a thing until then.

"I'm ready to go," she said, the words stilted.

He nodded, not trusting himself to speak just now. There were things he had to come to terms with himself. Like the fact that his career would add an element of risk to his child's life...damn. He hadn't wanted it to happen this way.

After stopping at the desk to sign out and pick up instructions for the treatment of a mild concussion, they walked in silence to his truck. Who would have thought that his life would be so different now? When he'd parked in this lot only a short while ago, Joe hadn't had a care in the world...not really.

But now...

He couldn't help glancing furtively at Lisa's flat belly. How long would it be before she began to look pregnant? He blinked and turned his attention back to opening the passenger door for her. He had no idea, but he would damn sure find out. There were books on the subject. He'd have to pick one up and find out all about pregnancy. He never liked going into anything blind. The idea rattled him.

Pregnancy. Fatherhood.

His whole life was about to change. He had eight months tops to retain his bachelor status.

His brain instantly calculated how many Thursday poker nights that included and how many Saturday-night dates that allowed, and then he remembered that everything had changed.

He had a new responsibility. He'd have to make adjustments to his old life.

Joe swallowed hard and pulled back out onto Washington Street, pointing his truck toward Lisa's home. His carefree bachelor days were over. He had to make some serious changes.

First and foremost he had to convince Lisa that he deserved to be a part of this baby's life. Of hers.

A frown creased his forehead. Wait a minute. Convincing her shouldn't be necessary. This baby was as much his as it was hers. She should simply tell him she was pregnant and they would work out a strategy for raising the child.

He waited for that to happen, but it didn't.

The only thing she said to him the entire journey was

that she wanted to go to her clinic rather than home so she could check on the animals.

He parked in the small lot that bordered the popular clinic. Everyone in Courage Bay loved Dr. Lisa and Dr. Greg. Joe rolled his eyes when he thought of Lisa's partner. The guy was one of those sissy sensitive types who never got his hands dirty and always looked properly pressed and styled.

Joe's gaze traveled down his own dusty, grimy appearance as he walked Lisa to the door of the clinic. The guy would never dream of crawling through shifting rubble to rescue anyone. He was too proper for that.

"I appreciate the ride," Lisa said, halting at the door without inviting him to come inside.

Joe shifted his concentration from thoughts of Greg. "You're sure you're okay?" he asked in a last-ditch effort to get her to confide in him. "Who'll take care of you tonight?" He remembered clearly that the doctor had said she needed someone with her.

"I'm fine," she insisted sharply. "I'm sure you have other things to do. Baby-sitting me any longer isn't necessary."

Well, at least she'd used the word *baby*. Just not in the context he'd wanted to hear. "You'll make sure you follow the doctor's instructions?"

"Yes," she agreed impatiently. "I'll get Kate to spend the night with me."

Kate was her sister, who would likely have her hands full if her home or her kids' school had suffered any damage.

"If Kate's busy, you go to your folks' place for the night," he insisted. He wanted her taking good care of herself. She was carrying his child, even if she hadn't told him yet. "You can call me, but I'll probably be out—"

"I'll be fine, Joe." She stared at him for a moment before continuing. He couldn't help wondering if she could see in his eyes that he knew her secret. "Whatever we shared was over weeks ago," she reminded him. "Unless you make it a practice to follow up on all your rescued victims, then I'd say you've already done more than enough."

Over. Whatever they'd shared was *over?*

The words kept ringing in his ears. How could she say that? But then he knew.

Lisa was as shaken by the news as he was. It would take time for her to come to terms with the reality herself. She wouldn't want to talk about it until she'd gotten used to the idea. He could understand that.

"All right then." He shrugged one shoulder as if it didn't matter. "Take care of yourself."

He reached for her…just to touch one soft cheek.

She drew away. "Thanks again for saving my life," she said. "I know how much you risked yourself. I really am grateful." Her gaze turned hard then. "But you always risk too much, Joe."

With that she turned and went inside, closing the door firmly behind her.

He stood there for a moment, trying to reason out why she'd made that last remark. Sure, he took calculated risks when the need arose. Where would she be if he hadn't?

Where would their baby be?

A shudder rocked through him. He didn't want to think about that.

And, by God, she'd better get used to him coming around and checking on her.

That baby was his.

CHAPTER FIVE

As soon as Lisa had ensured that the animals at her clinic were all safe, she'd picked up a rental car and gone home. Greg had insisted on doing the driving. Nancy Fowler, their reliable, ever-optimistic receptionist, had followed so that she could take Greg back to the office afterward. Greg and Nancy would stay at the clinic late, in the event anyone in the community needed emergency care for their pets.

Lisa, on the other hand, would be home, fretted over by her worried-but-relieved mother, who had insisted on coming to her aid the moment she heard the news. Now, despite a long, warm bath and a calorie-laden dinner only her mother would consider healing, Lisa still felt restless and incredibly at odds with herself. The whole situation felt like some sort of dream she couldn't wake from.

She sank deeper into the pillows her mother had stacked at the end of the sofa and pulled the cashmere throw up around her chin. She *so* did not want to think, but her brain just wouldn't shut down.

Her mother was in the kitchen cleaning. Lisa's oven was never as shiny as it could be, according to her meticulous mother. This time, rather than simply point out the deficiency, the generous master housekeeper had decided to clean it the *right* way. As if that weren't bad enough, her mother had gone on and on about Lisa's empty refrigerator. How was a girl supposed to keep up her strength with nothing but bottled water in her fridge? her mother lamented.

It was true. Lisa rarely used the stove, so she rarely cleaned it. She seldom cooked at home, since she spent so much time at the office, so why shop? It was easier to pick up something after work. Not fast food either. Several of the better local restaurants offered takeout. It was far simpler than attempting to prepare a decent meal for one. At least that's what Lisa told herself. It wasn't that she couldn't cook—okay, she wasn't that great at it. But who had the time? This, as her mother would point out, was a cardinal sin. All good Catholic girls knew how to cook.

Lisa sighed. Maybe the stove would keep her mother busy for a while. Lisa had answered about all the questions she could for one night. Any further discussion would risk a breakdown of her defenses.

She just couldn't tell her mother yet. It wasn't that she wouldn't be accepting and understanding…eventually. But how did you tell your mom that you were pregnant when you weren't married? Didn't even have a steady boyfriend? Lisa could just imagine her sweet, devoutly Catholic mother demanding to know who the errant father was and then, not so nicely, insisting that the perpetrator marry her daughter.

Nope. She definitely was not ready for that moment of truth.

She clicked off the television and tossed aside the remote. She'd seen all the news she could bear for one evening. Although the earthquake had not done as much damage as early reports indicated, each shot of crushed vehicles and caved-in roofs made Lisa wonder if Joe was still out there risking his life to rescue trapped victims.

When she raised a hand to her face, Lisa's fingers came away damp. She cursed her weakness. How could she have fallen so hard for such a thick-skulled, single-minded guy?

Joe loved his freedom, reveled in taking risks. What on earth had she been thinking? Her mother had always warned her against men like Joe. *They don't make good marriage material,* she had said. *Think, Lisa. What you want is a good, reliable model like your father.*

That was just it. The relationship between Joe and her had never involved thinking. It had been about fierce attraction, incredible sex. A shiver swept through her as she remembered. Not that she'd had much experience before Joe, but no one had ever made love to her like that. He made her very soul sing with desire.

She frowned, aware of the ache in her head. Closing her eyes, she tried to block out the pain but with no success. The mild pain reliever she'd taken obviously wasn't strong enough, but she didn't feel comfortable taking anything else. She'd just have to deal with it. Sleep would be a relief, if only she could turn off her thoughts. Her mother would wake her every couple of hours to make sure she was responding appropriately. Thankfully the nausea and dizziness had pretty much passed.

Yet no matter how she tried, she couldn't put Joe out of her mind. It would be so easy to pretend that the real attraction between them had been mere sex, but, unfortunately, that wasn't the way of it. Well, not from her side of things, anyway. Yes, the physical draw was relentless, but there was more. She loved looking at him, listening to him talk. His voice…mercy, what a voice. Deep, sensual and, oh, so masculine. The kind of voice that gave any woman in hearing distance goose bumps.

Tall, muscular, with thick, dark hair and equally dark eyes—and the way he moved. She sighed in surrender as her mind replayed moment after moment of the time she'd spent with him. It was more than just the deliberate, confident way he walked that was so appealing. There was an almost calculated efficiency to each flex of muscle. Every single thing about him beckoned to her on a purely female level.

The only thing that had stopped her from telling him the whole truth today was the knowledge that she needed to step back and look at the situation from a more objective angle. And she couldn't do that in Joe's presence. No matter how good he looked, how sweet he talked and how well he made love, he was not—repeat not—marriage material. Sadly, her mother was right on that score.

Unfortunately for Lisa, that was the bottom line.

Her first thought was that if Joe discovered the pregnancy, he would run like hell. But then she mulled over all that she knew about him. Her first assessment was wrong. Joe might love being single and playing the field, but he took responsibility very seriously. Maybe he wouldn't want to play the part of husband, but he would definitely want to be a father to *his* child.

That would end any hope for her as far as building a relationship with someone else was concerned. She covered her mouth to stifle the laugh that choked out of her. Who would want to risk life and limb to date the mother of Joe Ripani's child? No man would chance pissing off the Iceman.

God, she was doomed.

Though she would love this child, he or she would ultimately be the only one she ever had. Joe would see to that. While he frolicked with one female admirer after the other, Lisa would be sentenced to a life of utter loneliness and maternal exile.

That left her only one choice.

She could never tell Joe that the child was his. He couldn't control what he didn't know.

Before the idea could fully mesh in her brain, her heart objected. She couldn't do that to him.

"You all right, dear?"

Lisa jerked back to the here and now and focused on her mother's hovering form. She managed a nod. "I'm fine, Mom."

Ruth Malloy wasn't remotely convinced. Those keen blue eyes studied her daughter closely. "Are you sure, dear? I thought I heard you laughing in here. Then I thought maybe you were crying."

Lisa forced a smile. "No, really. I'm fine. I was just thinking, that's all."

Ruth sat down on the coffee table, facing Lisa. "You're sure I don't need to call the doctor. I know you're shaken, but this odd behavior just isn't like you." She wrung her hands anxiously. "You're so quiet…so distant. You're positive you're not injured worse than you're letting on? You'd tell me if the doctor mentioned anything besides a concussion."

Damn but the woman was good. Lisa took her mother's hands in hers and did the only thing she could. She avoided the truth. "I promise I would tell you if I were in pain or had any other injuries. And, yes, the whole episode was terrifying, but I'm safe." She sighed and looked away. "Some weren't as lucky as me." So far there had been more than a dozen deaths reported across the city. She prayed there wouldn't be any more.

"Praise our heavenly Father you're okay," her mother agreed. "Your sister and her family are safe, and your father and I are, as well." She looked around Lisa's cozy living room. "None of our homes were damaged. We were truly blessed." Her solemn gaze settled on her daughter once more. "Still, I can't help feeling that you're not telling me everything."

Her mother had always known when something wasn't as it should be, Lisa thought. It was as if the good Lord had blessed her with a kind of ESP where her daughters were concerned. Lisa and Kate had never been able to hide anything from her.

"Really, Mom, everything is fine," Lisa insisted, assuring herself it was only a white lie, one of many to come, no doubt. Her mother would know the facts soon enough. God, Lisa dreaded that moment. She remembered Kate's big church wedding. The white wedding dress. For purity, her mother had noted to anyone listening. Ruth Malloy still looked upon the holy state of matrimony the same way her own mother had more than half a century ago. She wasn't so blind to the ways of the modern world that she didn't know that people had sex before marriage all the time these days. But as long as her daughters didn't, she would not judge what the rest of the world did. Then there was the whole single-parent issue. Choosing to have children outside marriage was now completely acceptable in the eyes of many, but it was a huge no-no in the Malloy home.

Lisa suddenly felt very ill, and it had nothing to do with the bump on her head.

"Is it that young man? That fireman, Joe Ripani, who rescued you?" Her mother's gaze narrowed suspiciously. "You know I warned you about him," she chided. "Gladys Childers told me that his mother told her that he never stays with one girl for long. He goes from one to the next as if he's afraid there might be a shortage in the future and he has to get his fill now."

Lisa clamped down on her bottom lip to keep from smiling. This was not amusing, even if Gladys Childers was right. Courage Bay might be a thriving metropolis, but it was still amazing how many people knew each other. There were few secrets.

"I know you liked him a lot," Ruth went on. She adjusted the throw around Lisa's legs. "Not that I can blame you. He's a handsome man." She ushered Lisa into an upright position so she could fluff her pillows. "But he's a heartbreaker." She eased her daughter back into a reclining position. "Not to mention his work. They say he takes far too many risks. Turns off all emotion as if he thinks nothing of his own life."

"That's his job," Lisa pointed out. Not that she was taking Joe's side here. "If he didn't do his job, I might not be here right now."

"Well, now, you've got a point there," her mother allowed. "And I'm grateful to him. But what kind of life would that be for the woman who marries him? Always worrying that he wouldn't come home to you." She shook her head. "Why, how could you live like that? What you need is a good, reliable husband who considers the repercussions of what he's about to do before he acts. Like your father."

Lisa had heard this advice more times than she could remember. Careful, reliable. The most dangerous work her father ever did was write out a high-risk life insurance policy for a new client.

Ruth felt her daughter's forehead and then patted her hand. "No matter how much of a fire he sets in your soul, dear, it's the stability in the marriage that counts. Think what a fine life your father and I have had. Trust me, dear, stick with those men who are a bit more refined. Gladys has a nephew who just made vice president at the bank."

If Lisa hadn't already been depressed, she would

have been after this little pep talk. Of course, her mother had no way of knowing that it was far too late for Lisa to be worrying about such things now. She'd already fallen hard for Joe and she was carrying his child. Her future was no longer her own.

THE FIRST TWELVE HOURS after the quake were the most crucial. The last live rescue had occurred at 12:15 a.m., and so far only fourteen lives had been lost. To Joe's way of thinking, that was fourteen too many. And it would be weeks before the full extent of the property damage was known. None of the victims were friends of Joe's but one of the guys in his squad had known one of the victims discovered on the lower level of the parking garage. The vic, a Lance Corker, was a technician of some sort at Esmee Engines. Joe vaguely recognized the name of the company but had never heard of Corker.

The outpouring of support in the form of aid from surrounding communities had allowed for success in even the most technically challenging extrications. Now, nearly twenty-four hours after disaster struck, the secondary search was in full swing. Heavy equipment and canines from a dozen law enforcement agencies were on the job. The American Red Cross mobile disaster team had arrived and the Salvation Army was on hand to provide additional support.

Joe's squad, after working through the night, had been debriefed and ordered back to the station house for food and rest. Counseling sessions would come later. All emergency personnel were encouraged to discuss their disaster experiences to help head off post-traumatic stress disorder.

Property-damage assessment had begun at daybreak. Teams of engineers would evaluate every structure, even those seemingly untouched by the quake, for stress damage. Nothing would be left to chance.

Joe pushed himself up from his bunk. No way could he sleep a minute longer. Three hours was enough. He was itching to call Lisa. Just to make sure she was okay, he assured himself. But that was a lie.

He wanted to give her another chance to tell him that she was pregnant.

With his child.

But he couldn't bring himself to make the call.

All night long, even during the most complicated rescues, some part of his thoughts was on her. Was she okay? Was the baby okay? Surely Dr. Winslow would have checked out all the possibilities. That was probably what all the blood work had been about.

Then again, he had told her to see an obstetrician. Maybe there was some question in his mind.

Joe shook off that idea. He felt certain the doc would have admitted Lisa to the hospital if he'd been worried about the pregnancy in any way, especially considering the trauma she'd just gone through.

He ran his fingers through his hair. He was restless. Damn restless. He couldn't sit still. Couldn't stop thinking about her. The only thing he could come up with to do was to get an update on the rescue efforts and jump in to help out. He'd had all the rest he needed.

But first he had to have some coffee. Maybe a strong dose of caffeine would clear his head.

Joe slowed outside the kitchen. He didn't make it a habit of eavesdropping, in spite of the fact that he'd done just that at the hospital yesterday. Generally he didn't pay much attention to other people's business. That's the way he liked it. If he didn't nose around in their affairs, they wouldn't nose around in his.

But when he heard Lisa's name mentioned, he stopped near the kitchen door. The firehouse kitchen served as a gathering place more often than not.

"I'll let you know," O'Shea was saying to Spike and Bull. "I'm having lunch with Lisa later this afternoon."

So O'Shea and Lisa were having lunch.

Joe decided that maybe he wouldn't have to call Lisa to find out how she was doing after all. O'Shea would tell him. A grin slid across his face. A little reverse psychology and he'd get all the info he needed. Maybe enough to devise an excuse to drop by and see her, giving her that chance to come clean with him.

Satisfied that he had the situation under control, Joe followed the smell of rich, freshly brewed coffee. He didn't know why he'd ever worried. He could handle Lisa. She would see this his way, he was certain of it.

THINGS WENT DOWNHILL for Lisa.

She'd scarcely slept at all the night before.

Her mother had made a big breakfast that Lisa couldn't eat. Not with her stomach twisting and undulating with equal parts dread and anxiety. She thought it was too early for morning sickness, but she wasn't sure. And she couldn't ask her mother or her sister. At this point she couldn't talk to anyone.

The entire day, she'd alternated between joy and panic. Surely this emotional roller coaster wasn't good for the baby. She had to find a way to get herself under control.

She'd called the obstetrician's office and made an appointment, then picked up the vitamins that Brad had prescribed. Even the pharmacist had seemed to look at her with curiosity, though she was likely imagining it, the result of her own self-doubts.

Tears brimmed on her lashes yet again. This was so silly. She couldn't walk around like this, taking out her irritation on the rest of the world. What would people think? She had patients to see. And with patients came their owners. No one knew her secret yet. Why couldn't she get that fact through to her emotions?

Hormones.

The realization struck like a sudden summer storm. Well, of course. Her hormones were fluctuating, causing her extreme highs and lows.

If she remembered correctly, that problem would pass eventually. There wasn't a hell of a lot she could do about it. With that in mind, she called in her next patient.

Four dogs, two guinea pigs and one cat later, Lisa had to take a break. She'd promised Shannon they would have lunch this afternoon, but she wasn't sure she could hold out until then without eating something. Her stomach felt far too queasy to risk the wait.

The waiting area was finally clear, but she knew from experience that it would fill up again by two or three that afternoon. People were trying to go about their usual business, and most of the appointments were for vaccinations and checkups. Lisa had seen only one earthquake-related patient, a dog who'd been trapped in a collapsed storage building. Lucky for him, he'd come out of the ordeal without injury. Two closely spaced pillars of concrete blocks had formed a protective enclosure. Still, his master had wanted him checked out just to be sure.

After letting Nancy know she planned to take a short break in her office, Lisa grabbed a pack of snack crackers and a juice box from the small kitchenette that served as a staff lounge and retreated to her private office.

Dropping into the chair behind her desk, she quickly ripped opened the crackers. By the time she'd downed half of them, plus the juice, she felt better, her tummy settling down. Greg was probably having lunch in his office, too. He and Lisa rarely ate together, mostly because Lisa didn't want to encourage him. Greg Seaborn was a terrific partner. The best. He was a little older than her—thirty-one—and had the absolutely best bedside manner. Everybody loved him. He was so good with the animals. Nothing ever seemed to test his patience. Even Lisa became irritated from time to time, usually with an owner rather than a pet. But not Greg. He was easygoing and good-natured to the end.

And he had a huge crush on her.

Lisa heaved a sigh. Greg truly was a terrific guy. So

nice and really cute. She wouldn't actually call him muscular, but he was trim and athletic looking. He rode his bike to work every day. His sandy-colored hair was always neatly combed. Even the gold, wire-rimmed glasses didn't detract from his pleasant face or those warm green eyes.

Greg was thoughtful. He never forgot her birthday. His manners were impeccable. They had a world of interests in common. Both loved animals—any kind. Horseback riding and biking. Soft rock and pop music. Slow dancing. Art. Museums. Even the occasional game of golf.

As if that weren't enough, they attended the same church. Every Sunday he would wave to her as she took her seat next to her mother.

And he adored Lisa.

So what was the problem?

She closed her eyes and tried to slow the sudden spinning in her head. She shouldn't be doing this. She should be resting her mind, as well as her body. Why put herself through this torture?

Because of the baby.

This child needed a mother and a father. A stable home.

She couldn't help thinking about her own childhood. Sure, there were ups and downs in any family, but her parents stood by each other, were true to each other, and were always there for their children. Together.

Every child should have a home life like that.

Her hand went instinctively to her abdomen. Would her child have a life like that?

The answer was up to her, wasn't it?

Life with Joe Ripani would be anything but calm and steady—more like a roller-coaster ride.

Yes, he made her blood boil. Yes, he was a good man. But he just wasn't marriage material, and definitely wasn't father material.

Not like…Greg.

The tears came before she could stop them. Not a quiet-flow-down-the-cheeks kind either. She actually sobbed out loud. She couldn't stop herself. The emotions just burst from her as if she were ten all over again and had fallen from the tree house she and Kate had fashioned in their favorite tree. Lisa's arm had been broken and the pain had been nearly unbearable for a child. Her mother had comforted her with sweet words and soft assurances on the way to the hospital, and by the time they arrived at the E.R., her father had been there, as well. A safety net. A security blanket. Love and support. She'd never had to worry.

Until now.

She grabbed a handful of tissues as another flood of tears threatened.

"Lisa."

Greg. Oh God.

"I'm fine," she managed to say hoarsely. She blew her nose and blotted her tears with a wad of tissue. "Really," she said, not making eye contact. "I'm fine."

He was behind her desk and crouched next to her before she could suck in a ragged breath.

"No, you're not." He pushed the hair behind her ears.

"Talk to me, Lisa. After yesterday's trauma, it's not unusual to feel emotional. You were almost killed. You just need to talk it out."

She looked at him then. There was genuine concern in those kind eyes. He did care. He was such a good guy. Why couldn't she have fallen for him instead of…? God, she didn't even want to think his name.

The baby.

His baby.

How would she ever provide the right kind of home for this child? A kid needed both a mother and father. But could she…could this child survive Joe Ripani? Her heart squeezed at the idea that even now he was likely out there risking his life for someone else's.

"Please, Lisa," Greg urged softly, "talk to me. You know I'm always here for you."

And that was the bottom line.

She needed dependable.

Joe couldn't in a million years give her that.

"Oh, Greg, I've really made a mess of things," she admitted, her breath catching miserably. She was such an idiot. "I can't believe I let this happen."

He stood, reached for the box of tissues and offered it to her. When she'd taken it, he settled on the edge of her desk and waited for her to explain.

"Okay," she said, taking a deep, bolstering breath. She couldn't keep this a secret. Greg would know eventually. Everyone would, once she began to show.

Greg was her partner here. She owed him the truth. Summoning every ounce of courage she possessed, she settled her gaze on Greg's expectant one and said, "I'm pregnant."

To his credit, he didn't allow the shock he must have felt to show. He simply said, "I take it you just learned this at the hospital yesterday."

She nodded.

"Everything is all right?" he asked, concern in his voice.

She nodded again. "I…I just don't know what to do…" Closing her eyes, she shook her head. "How could I have let this happen?"

"Do you want the child?" he asked gently.

Her eyes shot open. "Of course."

But then he must have known that would be her answer. His sad smile attested to that knowledge. He reached for her hand and patted it soothingly. "It'll be all right, Lisa. You'll make a wonderful mother. You have a kind, supporting family." He squeezed her hand with firm confidence. "Everything will be fine. You'll see."

Another sound of anguish burst from her and the tears started anew. She wasn't usually such a crybaby, but this…

"How can I do this alone?" The words poured out, as unstoppable as the tears. She sniffled and hugged her arms around herself. Would the other kids make fun of her child at school if he didn't have a father? Or had people's views on the matter changed enough that she wouldn't have to worry? "I can't believe I let this happen," she repeated. Where was the responsible person she'd always been?

His touch gentle but firm, he pulled her to her feet and

into his arms. For long minutes he simply held her that way, offering soothing words that everything would be fine. He made that same confident promise over and over.

When her emotional tirade had at last subsided and she drew back from his comforting embrace, she felt as embarrassed as hell. "I'm sorry," she muttered. "I didn't mean to fall apart on you." But he was the one person she could do just that with and have no regrets. She'd needed to spill it all out to someone.

"I understand. This is a big deal. An enormous change."

She nodded and wiped her cheeks with the backs of her hands.

"Joe Ripani is the father," he said carefully.

That was the other thing about Greg. He would never put anyone down. Even the man who'd gotten the woman he wanted for himself pregnant.

How could any guy be this nice?

She nodded again, feeling very much like a bobble-headed idiot. "I really screwed up, didn't I?" Greg knew Joe's reputation. No one could find fault with Joe's professional conduct, but when it came to women…

"We all make mistakes, Lisa," he said. "Don't beat yourself up. What's done is done. You want the child and that should be your focus now."

She sagged against the desk. "But how will I ever be able to do this? He'll…he'll make it so hard."

Greg would understand what she meant. Joe Ripani was a local hero, a legend almost, and utterly honorable. He would want to take care of his child.

"You have choices, Lisa."

The firmness of Greg's tone startled her and she looked up at him. "What do you mean?" Her head was starting to throb again. She needed another painkiller.

"Why does it have to be Joe?" Greg straightened from the desk, those green eyes more certain than she'd ever seen them. "Why not me? Why not choose me?"

"I…" She didn't get what he meant. "I don't understand."

"Marry me, Lisa. You know how I feel about you." He took her by the arms and held on tightly. "I care deeply for you. I'll care for this child just as much…as if it were my own. You have a choice here."

"You want to marry me?" she asked, stunned and clearly a little slow on the uptake. Why would he want her now?

He smiled. "In a heartbeat. Just say the word and we'll do this right. I will never let you or this child down."

Before she could manage to respond, he reiterated his proposal. "Marry me, Lisa."

CHAPTER SIX

WEDNESDAY MORNING brought a bright new start for Joe, as well as the shaken residents of Courage Bay. The sun shone like a big ball of fire in the blue sky, offering hope and flooding the recovering city with renewed optimism.

Everything would be okay. Life would go on.

He could almost hear that mantra with each breath he drew as he climbed into his truck and headed toward the station house. Though he was supposed to be on R & R—rest and relaxation—he intended to stop by and check on his buddies from the squad who were on call today. He'd heard that some of those guys had endured harrowing experiences similar to his after the quake. He needed to pass along the praise he felt swelling in his chest.

Courage Bay firefighters were the best. Especially those at Jefferson Avenue Firehouse.

The emergency services in the city had worked together like a well-oiled machine, and there was still much to do. But Joe felt confident that his team was ready to do its part.

After an adrenaline-pumping visit with his buddies, he intended to question O'Shea regarding her lunch date yesterday and then to confront Lisa about the baby.

She'd had plenty of time to come to terms with the news. A part of him was thoroughly disappointed that she hadn't at least called. But, he reminded himself, this was a *big* deal. A really big deal. Maybe she did need more time. He knew that Lisa didn't like making snap decisions. She preferred to consider all her options before making a move.

He grinned. Well, there had been one thing they'd never wasted time deliberating about.

Making love.

Neither of them had taken more than a split second to consider the repercussions of tearing each other's clothes off. Rational thought simply hadn't entered into the equation.

The memory alone elicited a near spontaneous combustion. Every muscle in his body turned to granite.

Joe blew out a tight breath. As phenomenal as the sex had been, he had to remember that behavior like that was not typical for Lisa. He had her personality nailed down.

And there was a hell of a difference between having sex and having a baby.

Still, he wasn't going to be left out of any decisions she might make.

A tinge of fear doused the heat simmering deep inside him. She wouldn't consider…

No way. Lisa would never do that. She loved children too much. He could see it in the way she interacted with the kids who brought their pets into her clinic. She would never in a million years consider terminating the pregnancy. She had far too much respect for life.

Though that didn't worry him, there were other decisions that had to be made. The kid would need a name and there was the question of who would take care of the baby while they worked. Lisa was as dedicated to her profession as he was to his. He'd heard his buddies talk about day-care dilemmas. Finding good care wasn't easy. His mother was a retired schoolteacher with plenty of free time.

Why not ask her?

His mom would definitely take good care of his kid, especially since it would be her first grandchild.

But maybe Lisa would want her own mother to do the child-care thing. Either one would be okay, he supposed.

And then there was the issue of religion. Lisa's family was Catholic and Joe's was Methodist.

Damn. That opened up a whole other can of worms. Where would the rugrat go to church on Sundays? Not that Joe went that often, but it was different with a kid. A kid needed proper spiritual guidance. A solid foundation.

And what about ball games and camping trips. Of course, that was down the road a ways, but what if Lisa married some other guy? Who would take his son to see the Angels win the World Series? Or head out to the mountains for his first camping trip? Fury roared inside Joe. It damn sure wouldn't be some other jerk. He clenched his jaw hard enough to crack the enamel of his teeth. No damn way.

Joe braked for a traffic light. Then again, the baby could be a girl. Girls needed dance lessons and dolls. Worry seared into his skull. He didn't know anything about dance lessons and dolls. Hell, the only thing he knew about dance was that a ballerina wore a tutu and looked like a fairy. And did a Barbie count as a real doll?

Then there would be boys and dating.

A new kind of rage mushroomed in his chest. Who would protect her from all those boys? He knew what boys had on their minds 24/7. Sex. Nothing but sex. Any boy who tried to have sex with his daughter would die a seriously painful death, by God.

A horn blasted behind him, dragging Joe from his blood pressure–raising ruminations. Just let some boy try to touch his daughter.

He stomped the accelerator and rocketed through the intersection. There would be rules for dating his little girl. Strict rules.

Joe was at the end of the next block before he noticed the blue lights throbbing in his rearview mirror. He swore and eased over to the curb. Shaking his head, he called himself every kind of fool as he lowered the driver's-side window. He'd probably been speeding while worrying about the daughter he didn't even have yet.

Jeez, if it was this bad now, how the hell would he survive when the kid actually got here?

"Good morning," the traffic cop commented dryly as he strolled up to the window. "Where you headed in such a hurry this morning?"

It took Joe a full two minutes to talk his way out of

a ticket. He had a feeling that if the officer hadn't re-membered Joe's name from the rescue at the parking ga-rage, he'd have given Joe a ticket anyway. The pregnant woman who'd waited outside while her mother went to get the car had been the officer's wife.

"Just try to keep your mind on business while driv-ing, okay, Captain Ripani?"

Joe managed a smile and a vague nod. "Sure thing. Thanks for letting me slide this time."

When the officer started to walk away, Joe called after him. "Hey, do you have kids at home, besides the one on the way, I mean?" He didn't know what pos-sessed him to ask the question, but he suddenly needed to hear someone else's experience.

With a grin, the guy spun back around and whipped out his wallet to show off his brood.

He had two boys and one girl already. The one on the way was a girl, as well, according to the latest ultra-sound. And the last, he added succinctly.

"So, tell me," Joe ventured, scratching his head as he dredged up the courage to ask what he desperately needed to know. "Is having a kid—the first one espe-cially—is it hard?"

"Got one on the way, have you?"

Joe nodded uncertainly.

"It's the hardest thing you'll ever do, pal." He braced his hands on the roof of Joe's truck and leaned in a lit-tle closer as if what he was about to say was top secret. "But there's nothing else in the world like it. The sex department kind of goes to hell after kids come into the picture, but…" He shook his head. "There's no way to adequately describe how it feels when you see your child for the first time."

The radio clipped to his belt crackled and the officer straightened. "Well, gotta go." He gave Joe a thumbs-up. "Be safe now. Remember, kids learn by example."

For several minutes after the officer had gone, Joe just sat there in his truck. The guy's friendly advice had driven one point all the way home.

Everything in Joe's life was about to change.

The sex department kind of goes to hell kept ringing in his ears. But even more frightening was that final remark.

Kids learn by example.

What kind of role model would he be?

What if he did everything wrong?

Where was the manual on how to do this right?

Joe forced the thoughts from his head and checked the street so he could pull back into the flow of traffic.

His mood—his whole damn demeanor—wilted as he headed toward the station house.

He was going to be a father and he didn't have the slightest idea how to be a good one.

His old man had been a great guy. Though he'd passed on when Joe was a senior in high school, Joe had lots of great memories. He and his two brothers had never questioned their father's support. Joe's dad had been at every game, taken them camping, taught them to drive. His tragic death in a hotel fire while on a business trip was what had made Joe want to become a fireman.

And Joe wanted to be the best of the best, to ensure

that no one in his jurisdiction had to die like his father. Joe had wanted to make a difference.

He'd done what he'd set out to do. He was among the best of the best, just as the rest of his squad was. But could he be a good father?

That was the real question here.

And there was only one acceptable answer in Joe's opinion.

Damn straight he could be.

Things were a little calmer at the station this morning. Some members of the duty squad had already been called out for recovery detail.

Joe would prefer to be with them, but he knew the hazards of failing to get proper time off. Running on empty was a bad thing in this line of work. He'd learned that the hard way.

Making his way to the TV room, he drew up short as he rounded the corner.

"Whoa, almost had ourselves a head-on collision," he said to Shannon O'Shea, who'd practically run him over.

O'Shea was one lady who could likely do it, as well. She was every bit as tall as Joe, six feet at least. And she was strong, good-looking and athletic as hell. All anyone had to do was ask Nubs, the last firefighter she'd beat at arm wrestling. O'Shea wasn't called Biceps for nothing.

"Hey, Cap'n," she said breathlessly. "Didn't expect to see you here today." She averted her gaze and seemed anxious to be on her way.

Joe blinked. Was she acting suspicious or was it just

his imagination? "What about you? I didn't think I'd find you hanging around here today, either. What're you up to?" Actually, Joe wasn't surprised to see O'Shea here. She was as bad as he was about dropping by on her off-duty days.

She made an attempt at a shrug. "I dunno."

Joe had a bad feeling that her evasiveness had something to do with Lisa. Why else would she be acting so strangely around him? Hadn't she been the one to give him down the road when he and Lisa parted ways? Yeah, she had. And it was old Biceps who was always telling the squad that her fiancé, FBI agent John Forester, had shown her how a man was supposed to treat a woman—a lesson the male squad members could benefit from. Hell, Joe had known with complete certainty that those barbs were intended for him. O'Shea hadn't liked him calling it quits with her good friend. That fact had never once affected their working relationship, but on a personal level, he knew O'Shea was gravely disappointed in him.

His gaze narrowed. Did she know about the pregnancy?

Had Lisa shared with O'Shea what she wouldn't share with him?

He swore under his breath.

O'Shea gave him a look. "Don't get your boxers in a wad. I just came by to talk to some of the guys." She jerked her head toward the TV room. "So what's up with you today, Cap'n?" she asked, purposely diverting the conversation. Her defenses were fully in place now. She wasn't giving anything away.

Oh, he'd been right.

She knew something.

He folded his arms over his chest and looked her dead in the eye. "How did lunch go with Lisa yesterday? She doing okay?"

O'Shea was the one blinking to hide her emotions this time. "She…uh…she's doing great."

"Really?" Joe shot her a doubtful look. "No lingering headache from the concussion? No aches and pains?"

God knew he had enough of his own. Nobody could accuse him of not being in shape. Hell, he ran five miles every morning, worked out in the weight room right here at the station house during his on-duty downtime, as well as most of his off-duty days. But even a person in great shape came away from a rescue like Lisa's with a few aches and pains. Even a bruise or two.

O'Shea gave another one of those indifferent shrugs. "She didn't mention anything. She looked great." She gave him a knowing look, glee suddenly dancing in her eyes. "She looked glowing, even."

Joe's annoyance morphed into panic. What the hell did she mean by that? And why the sudden about-face? Two seconds ago she'd clearly been hiding something. Now she seemed ready to flaunt whatever she knew right in his face.

"Great," he snorted. "Glad she's okay."

He wasn't about to give O'Shea the pleasure of whatever smart-ass comeback she had planned for him next. Let her keep her little secrets. An uneasiness he couldn't explain had him anxious to move on.

"See ya around, O'Shea," he said as he gave her his back. Let her play this game with somebody else. It wasn't like her to gloat, but, admittedly, she was only human. If Lisa had chosen to share her news with her friend and not him, there was nothing he could do about that. He would have his time soon enough. Like today.

"Guess you didn't hear," O'Shea called to his retreating back.

Later, when he had cooled down enough to think about it, Joe wouldn't be able to say precisely what it was that made him turn around and face that challenging remark when every instinct warned him to keep walking. He only knew that something in O'Shea's voice wouldn't let him do that.

"Guess I didn't," he retorted.

"Lisa's getting married," she said, the smile lacing the words only making them sharper, cutting right to the bone. "Next week. She and Greg don't want to wait a minute longer."

Joe didn't remember leaving the station house. He only had one goal in mind. Getting the truth out of Lisa.

There was no way in hell she was going to marry Greg Seaborn. That had to be a bad joke she and O'Shea had come up with to play on Joe.

He gave the key in the ignition of his truck a violent twist and the engine roared to life. No way would Lisa marry a loser like Seaborn. Hell, she'd always treated the guy like a brother. Not that Joe had missed the way Seaborn looked at her. He thought she was amazing. Wanted her something bad. But Lisa had never given him anything but professional respect and friendly affection.

No way would she marry him.

As Joe maneuvered his truck into the morning traffic, another reality broadsided him.

She was pregnant with *his* child.

That made it impossible for her to consider marrying anyone else at this stage…didn't it?

Maybe not.

Panic slithered up his spine.

That might even be the reason she'd decided to do such a fool thing. Maybe she didn't want to have this baby alone. Maybe she thought she could marry Seaborn and pass the child off as his. O'Shea wouldn't lie. No way. If she said Lisa was getting married, then she was. Why hadn't he realized what this really meant?

As Seaborn's wife, Lisa wouldn't have to worry about Joe interfering. She and Seaborn would raise the child. Joe's son or daughter would call Seaborn *Daddy*.

Like hell.

He gunned the engine, forgetting the traffic cop's advice. No way in hell could he take the time to be cautious right now. Not when another man was trying to take his place with his own kid and the woman…the woman carrying his child.

An alien emotion, something teetering between fury and jealousy, ripped through Joe's chest. No one was going to take his place.

That baby was his. He wasn't about to let Lisa make this kind of rash decision.

What was she thinking?

Seaborn might be a nice, steady guy…

And there it was in a nutshell.

Nice. Steady. All the things a woman like Lisa looked for in a man.

Joe gritted his teeth. He wondered if the guy could make her scream his name the way Joe had? Wondered if he could make her beg for more the way Joe had? Joe would bet everything he owned that Greg Seaborn had never even kissed Lisa, much less made love to her.

Not the way Joe had, anyway.

He'd been there. Remembered the way she came apart in his arms. The way her body responded to his.

Greg Seaborn didn't deserve Lisa and he damn sure wasn't going to raise Joe's child.

Not as long as Joe was still breathing.

Joe might be thankful for a nice, steady guy like Seaborn if he were to die before he could do the job himself—before he could raise his child. But Joe was here, ready and willing. No one was going to take that privilege away from him.

This was his kid.

"EASY NOW," Lisa said cajolingly to the big collie. Naomi, as her nine-year-old owner called her, had managed to get herself into a fight with a stray dog that wandered into her territory. Thankfully her shots were up to date. Still, she would need to be quarantined for a few days. Since Lisa knew the family well, she had agreed to let the dog be quarantined at home. No going outside without a leash. But right now, she had a couple more stitches to add before she could send the collie home.

"I betcha there won't be any more strays coming into our yard," Timmy said as he stroked Naomi's back.

"Maybe not," Lisa said. The humane society had picked up the stray, but Lisa intended to go by and check him out herself. He might turn out to be a good dog that needed nothing more than a loving family like Timmy's to care for him. She made it her business to find that very kind of family for animals in need.

"Mom said Naomi was protecting me," Timmy told her, as if his mother weren't standing right behind him. "Maybe that stray would have bitten me."

"Maybe," Lisa agreed. "It's best to avoid animals you're unfamiliar with."

Timmy nodded. "Mom said I did the right thing by running into the house when I saw that dog."

Lisa glanced at his mother and smiled. "Your mom's a smart lady."

The sound of raised voices interrupted whatever Timmy would have said next.

Lisa frowned. Who on earth…? Male. Loud. It couldn't be Greg. He was on a house call this morning. Besides, Greg never yelled like that.

Then the voices sounded closer, and recognition hit her as if she'd slammed, full speed, into a brick wall.

"I want to see her now!"

Joe Ripani.

Timmy's mother looked startled, and Naomi made a distressed sound.

"Who's yelling?" Timmy asked, staring toward the closed door of the treatment room.

Lisa didn't have time to answer his question before the door burst inward and Joe's towering form filled the opening.

"We're a little busy in here," Lisa said to him with a pointed glare. Naomi growled deep in her throat, so Lisa stroked her soothingly.

"I'm sorry, Lisa," Nancy said, peeking around Joe's broad shoulder. "He insisted on seeing you *now.*" She looked apologetic and utterly flustered.

"It's okay, Nancy."

Shaking her head, the receptionist headed back to the front desk.

Joe's face was beet red and he appeared ready to do battle. With Lisa most likely. One glance at Timmy and his mother, and he relaxed his fighting stance just a little.

"I need to talk to you," he told her between clenched teeth. "Now."

Doing her level best to stay calm on the outside, Lisa met that savage glower and said, "Give me about ten minutes and I'll be with you. You can wait in my office, *Mr. Ripani.*"

She said his name with all the disdain she could muster. Thankfully he did as she asked, closing the door behind him. Rolling her eyes, she turned back to the business at hand. How dare he storm into her clinic like this! He had no right to behave in this manner.

The baby.

No. He couldn't know about the baby. No one other

than Greg did. She hadn't even told Shannon. She'd wanted to. God, she wanted to talk to someone besides Greg. But she just couldn't bring herself to talk about it yet with anyone else.

The wedding.

Her eyes rounded. God. He'd likely heard about the wedding.

Confusion made her head ache, reminding her that she had not fully recovered from the concussion just yet. Why would he care if she married Greg?

It didn't make sense.

Joe didn't want commitment or marriage. He'd walked away from her three weeks ago easily enough. Why would he care if she married someone else now?

Forcing the whole business aside, Lisa finished up with Naomi. "There," she said softly to the old dog. "What a good girl you were." Lisa turned to Timmy's mother. "Keep the sutures clean and dry, and bring her back in about ten days for the follow-up." She mussed Timmy's hair. "And don't worry, Naomi's fur will grow back as she heals."

Lisa scratched Naomi behind the ears and then helped her down from the table. The dog had been so cooperative a sedative hadn't been necessary. Just a local anesthetic. All repairs should be this easy.

Lisa accompanied the little entourage to the reception area, where she asked Nancy to give her a few minutes. While she tidied the treatment room and washed up, Lisa readied herself for the coming confrontation with Joe. She didn't know why she had to do this, but she did. He had no claim on her, as far as he knew. And he definitely had no right sticking his nose in her social life. The two of them were no longer an item. Whatever had put a burr under his saddle was his problem.

Lisa paused outside the door to her office and took a deep breath. This shouldn't take long. Joe would say whatever he had to say and then he'd go.

Men like Joe were like that. All bluster when it came to staking claims. He didn't really want her on a permanent basis. He was probably just miffed that she'd apparently gotten over him so fast.

If only he knew.

She stepped into her office and closed the door behind her. Hands braced on hips, Joe turned to face her.

"Why the hell are you marrying Seaborn?" he demanded with all the gruffness of an injured lion.

Lisa didn't say anything right away, choosing instead to tidy her desk and check her messages. She desperately needed to proceed with caution.

"Damn it, don't ignore me," he growled, planting both hands firmly on her desk and leaning toward her in a blatant act of intimidation.

She set her messages aside and met his furious gaze. Lord, his eyes were as dark as midnight when he was angry. Chasing the foolish thought from her mind, she said what had to be said. "We were over weeks ago, Ripani. What I do and with whom I do it is none of your business. Greg and I have been close for some time. We've simply decided to take it to the next level."

Something flickered in Joe's eyes, making her heart

gallop with remembered heat. "Has he made love to you the way I did?"

Now, that made her angry. How dare he call it making love! "You mean, have we had savage sex?" And that's what it had been, barbaric almost. Even knowing that it had been purely physical, Lisa felt a bolt of searing desire just at the thought of him driving into her.

The smoldering sensuality in his eyes blazed into all-out fury. "You don't want to marry him and you know it."

Her mouth dropped open. The gall of the man. "And how would you know?"

He reached across the desk and wrapped his long fingers around her neck, pulling her face close to his. Traitorously, her heart rate tripped as a rush of fire raced deep into her belly. The feel of his hot breath on her lips made her want to tilt her mouth toward his…made her long for his kiss.

"Because I know you—all of you," he murmured silkily. "So don't try any funny business with me."

Railing at herself mentally, she jerked away from him. "You are so full of yourself, Ripani." She was doing the right thing. If she'd had any second thoughts, they'd all disappeared. "I'm getting married next week whether you like it or not."

Joe straightened to his full height and squared those awesome shoulders. "I've played this your way long enough. I gave you every opportunity to come clean with me and you haven't. Now we're going to do this my way."

Panic flooded her. He couldn't know about…

"That baby you're carrying is mine. I know it and you know it." He stabbed a finger in her direction. "You should have leveled with me, Lisa." This time there was something more in his voice, something wounded. But how could that be? This was Joe Ripani. He didn't feel that kind of pain. And how had he found out about her secret?

"You could have told me when we left the hospital, but you didn't. Then I gave you time." He took a breath and visibly struggled to keep his voice civil. "Still you didn't tell me. Then I hear about this wedding. What am I supposed to think?"

She shook her head, causing pain to shoot in a dozen directions inside her skull. "First I want to know how you found out." The words came out almost as a shout. She hadn't meant to lose her grip, but he wasn't making it easy.

"I heard Winslow tell you," he said quietly, those wide shoulders sagging in resignation.

Why did he seem disappointed? It didn't make sense. None of this made sense. Oh, yes, it did, she suddenly realized. Responsibility. How could she have forgotten? He would see this baby as *his* responsibility. The idea of another man taking his place would be unthinkable.

"Don't do this, Joe," she warned, suddenly weary. "You know you don't want to be tied down. Just let me handle this the best way for the baby."

Renewed anger flamed in his eyes. "*My* baby," he reminded her none too gently. "No way am I going to let Seaborn be a daddy to my kid. No way, Lisa. Forget it!"

Lisa collapsed into her chair and braced her elbows on the desk. "And what would you have me do?" she asked. "Raise a child alone? Deprive him or her of the kind of stability you and I both enjoyed growing up?" She didn't have to go into the details. He would know what she meant.

He didn't answer right away. Shoving his fingers through his hair, he paced the small area in front of her desk for what felt like a mini-eternity. She could almost see the wheels turning in that handsome head. There was just no telling what kind of solution he would come up with.

Then he stopped and aimed that determined gaze back on her. "This is my baby, too. I have some say in the matter."

She didn't bother disagreeing. The baby was his. To lie to him would only make bad matters worse, and she knew she couldn't bring herself to go that far. She'd known she would have to tell him the truth eventually.

"I'll give you that, but why would you want any say?" She spread her hands out in genuine bewilderment. "Joe, you love being single. Why would you want to be tied down with a child?"

He blinked, clearly startled by her simplistic analysis. "Because it's the right thing to do."

The reality of that statement shook her. This was about more than responsibility. She couldn't say how much more, but there was something he wouldn't let her see.

Please don't let me be fooling myself, she prayed. Her heart so wanted to believe that he cared about her on a deep enough level that this was about her, too. Not just the baby.

"So what do you propose?" she asked.

Even as she posed the question, Lisa could not imagine what his answer would be. She'd considered several scenarios in the time since she'd learned about the pregnancy, always coming back to the one that had him popping in to see his child whenever he felt the urge and her being left in the cold by his heroic reputation and formidable possessiveness.

"Marry me," he said flatly. "I'm the child's father. It makes perfect sense." He planted his hands at his waist as if she should see his suggestion for what it was: the only right thing to do.

To say his reaction took her by surprise would have been a vast understatement. She mentally pinched herself to make sure she wasn't dreaming.

This was insane. Totally crazy.

Joe Ripani proposing marriage?

Impossible.

Admittedly, the proposal left a lot to be desired by any standards, but the sheer idea that he would ask made it almost—*almost* being the key word—endearing.

"Let me think about it."

Now they were even. Because her answer had just shocked the hell out of him.

CHAPTER SEVEN

WHEN JOE HAD GONE, Lisa wilted back into her chair.

How was she supposed to do this?

The choice had been so much easier when only one option was available besides doing this on her own. Greg would make a great father and a caring husband. Over the past twenty-four hours, she'd come to terms with her decision.

Now, the future she'd seen so clearly was muddied by Joe's proposal.

Joe didn't want to get married. She knew that with complete certainty. So why would he make such an offer?

For the baby, of course.

That's why she had insisted on taking some time to think about his proposal. She'd done it for his sake. He needed to think about it. He'd likely rushed over here and made the offer as soon as he discovered she planned to marry Greg. If, as he said, he'd overheard Dr. Winslow confirming her pregnancy, he certainly hadn't asked her then.

Anger simmered inside her. No. He hadn't been worried then. It wasn't until he heard that someone else had moved in on what he perceived as his territory that he came running over here to make his mark.

Men! She rolled her eyes. They could be such primitive jerks.

A light rap on her door dragged her from the male-bashing session she had mentally begun.

She sighed. Greg wasn't like that. He had just appeared in her door, waiting to be invited in. Greg would never attempt to *mark* anything as his, especially not another human being. He acted on intellect rather than instinct.

And she felt so relaxed when she was around him.

Why, then, was she even considering Joe's offer?

Because he was the father of this child. Like it or not, he would be involved. Not that she had wanted to exclude him. It was easy to sit here and pretend she might have kept him in the dark for his own good, but her conscience would have gotten the better of her eventually.

Unfortunately, she'd taken on the role of good girl in this life. Keeping his child a secret from him wasn't something she could do—even if it would make life a hell of a lot less stressful.

"He knows about the wedding, I take it," Greg guessed as she motioned for him to come in.

"He knows."

"About the baby, too?"

She nodded, not trusting herself to speak. Now that the adrenaline rush of Joe's abrupt visit had receded, she felt on the verge of tears. She gave herself a mental shake. All these tears were not like her. She'd thought she was stronger than this. Pregnancy hormones. And hers were likely amplified by her predicament.

"He overheard the doctor tell me at the hospital."

Greg quirked an eyebrow. "And he didn't mention this to you until now?"

A part of her felt guilty talking about Joe this way behind his back, especially with Greg. But the rest of her felt he deserved this and more.

"He heard about our…plans."

Greg settled into one of the chairs flanking her desk. "From the tone of his voice, I'd say he wasn't pleased."

"Not at all." Her partner had obviously returned from his house call in time to hear part of Joe's outburst.

Greg leaned forward, his green eyes filled with concern. "I hope he didn't upset you too much. If you need to go home for a while, I understand."

This was too much. How was she supposed to deal with all this? Joe insisting she marry him and Greg being so kind. Too kind. The two men were polar opposites.

Anxiety surged, making her heart beat faster. What was the right thing to do? She thought of the baby's need to know his or her biological father, but it was equally important for her child to have a stable home life. Then she thought of her own happiness.

She closed her eyes. She just didn't know what to do.

"Take some time, Lisa." Greg stood, and she looked up at him. "Don't try to make a decision now. Consider the facts and what you feel will make both you and the baby happy." His expression was full of tender concern.

"Don't let either of us push you into a decision that isn't what you really want."

Was he for real?

She watched Greg walk out of her office, leaving her more confused than before. How would she ever make this decision?

JOE PULLED INTO the driveway of his childhood home and sat there for about ten minutes before he worked up the nerve to get out. He needed to talk to someone about this. Someone he could trust—someone who had the right experience to draw upon.

Who better than his own mother?

He rapped on the kitchen door and waited for her to call out a familiar *come in.*

He smiled when her pleasant voice echoed through the brick rancher just as he'd known it would. He could always count on his mom.

The mouthwatering aroma of cookies baking had him peeking into the oven. Chocolate chip, his favorite. As if she'd known he was coming. He shook his head. How was it mothers always knew when their kids were in need? He wondered if that gift came automatically. And then his thoughts instantly went to Lisa and his child. Would she sense when his baby needed her?

Sure she would.

Lisa would make a wonderful mother. Why hadn't he noticed that before? Because a wife and kids hadn't been in his five-year plan.

"Hey, Ma." He bent down and pressed a kiss to her temple before she could get out of her chair to greet him.

"I had a feeling you'd be coming this morning," she said knowingly. She assessed him with one thorough glance, using that schoolteacher scrutiny that seemed to be second nature to her, even though she was retired.

"Is that so?" He settled onto the sofa opposite her and surveyed the strewn scrapbooks and related paraphernalia. Since retiring, his mother had gotten into scrapbooking. She insisted that it was for posterity. Joe wondered if it was more about not getting bored. She had her weekly bridge game and the garden club, but those activities didn't appear to be enough to keep her mind off the fact that her life's mate was gone. Teaching had done that for a long time, but Joe sensed that retirement had brought too many empty hours to miss his dad.

"Quite," she affirmed. "Your friend at the firehouse—Shannon, I believe her name is—called and said you might need a shoulder to lean on."

Ire shot through Joe so fast he almost jumped to his feet with the force of it. What the hell was O'Shea doing prying into his affairs? And how the hell had she known how upset he was?

Joe had a sneaking suspicion that a lot of people at the station would see Lisa's sudden nuptials to another man as a blow to his ego, even though he'd been the one to end their relationship. Did people really see him as that shallow?

He didn't like the answer—or the guilt—that echoed

all the way through him. O'Shea would be worried
about him. As annoyed as she was at him for hurting her
best friend, she still cared for and respected her captain.
He knew that. Still, that she had anticipated his feelings
on this matter irritated him. Maybe he *was* shallow
when it came to this kind of thing.

"Damn," he muttered.

His mother's eyebrows rose. "Pardon me?"

"Sorry." He flared his hands uncertainly. "I was just
thinking aloud."

"You know, son, going to church now and then
wouldn't hurt. Your brothers come every Sunday with
their wives. You're the only one in the family who
doesn't seem to find the time."

Oh, Lord. He should have known that talk was
coming.

"But then, you didn't come here to discuss your spiritual needs." She set aside the pictures she was attempting to arrange on a page. "It's about our lovely
veterinarian, I'm told."

He clenched his jaw and made a mental note to have
a long talk with O'Shea. Even if she thought she'd done
him a favor, this was pushing it. "In a roundabout way,"
he said.

His mother waited patiently for him to say more. That
always drove him crazy. She could outwait Job when she
knew one of her sons was withholding information.

Finally he broke down and gave her what she
wanted—the truth. "Lisa's partner at the clinic asked her
to marry him. I have a problem with that."

"I thought the two of you broke up," his mother ventured. "The way I hear it, you weren't interested in getting serious and Lisa was."

If O'Shea had told his mother that little detail, he was going to—

"That's true," he responded when she gave him one of those pointed looks that meant she expected an answer posthaste.

"Well, I just don't see the problem then. You weren't interested, Dr. Seaborn is." She shrugged. "There's an old saying, son, that's quite appropriate in this case. *You snooze, you lose.*"

He couldn't believe his own mother had just made such a smug, heartless remark to him!

"It's not that simple," he snapped before he could catch himself.

She studied him a moment, those dark eyes boring into him as if she had X-ray vision. She probably knew his next thought before he did. "Why don't you elaborate, since, God knows, I'm not psychic?"

Could have fooled him.

"You heard Lisa was trapped in that parking garage and I rescued her, right?" His mother nodded. "I wanted to make sure she was okay, so I took her by the E.R. afterward. I overheard Dr. Winslow when he gave her the results of all her tests." Now for the hard part. He blew out a heavy breath and blurted the rest. "Hetoldhershewaspregnant." He didn't even pause between the words.

Now, that got his unflappable mother's attention. She

opened her mouth to utter some profound statement just as the oven timer dinged.

"That'll be the cookies."

She got up and headed toward the kitchen before he could gather his scattered wits.

Knowing she would take the cookies from the oven and transfer them to the cooling rack before she returned, he pushed himself up from the sofa and wandered toward the kitchen. He needed her advice, no matter how much her disappointment in him would hurt.

He'd never let his mother down. He'd always managed to keep his grades up and behave himself—or at least be smart enough never to get caught. Now, here he was a grown man and he'd done the unthinkable.

Standing there in the kitchen he'd eaten breakfast in every day of his life until he graduated high school, he felt six years old again. And utterly helpless at the prospect of being forced to go to school. He'd hated kindergarten and felt certain first grade would be no better. His mother had known all the right things to say to set his mind at ease and boost his confidence.

He sure as hell hoped she had some pearls of wisdom to share now.

When the cookies were safely on the cooling rack and the baking sheet in the sink, she turned to her youngest son and totally blew his mind in very much the same way Lisa had when she'd told him she needed to think about his offer.

"No wonder Lisa agreed to marry Greg," she said.

"What is that supposed to mean?" His mother should

be on his side! There were some things a guy should be able to depend on.

"It means that when you learned about the pregnancy, you should have told her then and there that you knew and were fully prepared to accept responsibility for your actions. Not in those exact words, of course, but you should have made her aware that you were there for her."

Joe grunted in exasperation. "I was waiting for her to tell *me*. She didn't even know I knew when she accepted Seaborn's proposal."

"My point exactly," his mother retorted. "You didn't care enough to let her know that you knew. Rather, you allowed her to stew in her own pot of worries until desperation forced her to take the only offer on the table."

This was *his* fault? How did she get to that twisted conclusion?

"She should have told me," he insisted.

"Joe." His mother patted his shoulder as if he were a slow learner for whom she felt sympathy. "I love you. You're my son, but as far as I can tell, you haven't given Lisa or any other woman the first indication that you're interested in settling down. She likely assumed that a life with a reliable man like Greg was better than an unhappy marriage with a man who didn't care for strings of any sort."

And therein lay the crux of the whole issue. Much as he hated to admit it, his sage mother was right. As he had known she would be.

Lisa had no reason to see him as the husband-and-father type. She knew how he felt about strings and long-term commitment. She'd made the only choice she thought she could.

This was his fault, and somehow he had to make it right.

No way was Seaborn raising his child…no way was he having Lisa, either.

Joe would give her the time she asked for, but one way or another, he would show her that she could count on him. He could do the commitment thing. He could be a good husband, a reliable husband, just as easily as he could be a father.

All he had to do was prove it to her.

If she gave him the chance.

IT TOOK ALL of Lisa's courage the next morning to act on the decision she had reached.

She knocked on Greg's door long before she knew he would leave for the clinic. She didn't want to do this at work. The issue was far too personal.

He opened the door, his usual smile in place. "Good morning. You're out early."

"I need to talk to you, Greg."

His smile dimmed at her somber voice. "Come in." He stepped back and allowed her inside.

Lisa wrung her hands together, praying she was making the right choice for all concerned. When he'd closed the door, she moistened her lips and began her well-rehearsed speech.

"Greg, you don't know how much your proposal meant to me. I can't tell you—"

He held up a hand. "Don't do this to yourself, Lisa," he said, letting her off the hook. "I know why you're here."

A feeling of relief combined with a sense of defeat made staying vertical next to impossible. Her stomach roiled, forcing her to swallow.

"I…I don't want to hurt you," she said, knowing it was too late for that. This decision wouldn't be easy for Greg to accept.

He shook his head. "You haven't, not really. I knew from the moment you told me about the pregnancy that you'd end up with Joe." He lifted one shoulder in a resigned shrug. "It's where you belong. I can't compete with true love."

His statement startled her. "How…how did you know?"

He smiled. "Anyone could see how much you cared about him when the two of you were together. I knew. I just didn't want to admit it. When he walked away, I thought maybe I might have a chance after all. And then you learned about the pregnancy and I hoped I could be the knight in shining armor you would learn to love." He gave a slight grimace. "But that wasn't fair of me. I knew you were in love with him. I wanted you to know you had other options, but I don't want you to feel as if the choice you've made is wrong just because it's not the one I want to hear."

Tears spilled past her lashes. She just couldn't help it. "Greg, I'm only trying to do the right thing for this baby."

"You are doing the right thing. This is Joe Ripani's

child. You should try to make a marriage to him work. It is the right thing to do."

She couldn't stop herself—she had to hug him. He felt so steady, so caring. Why couldn't she have fallen in love with Greg?

"Just so you know," he murmured. "I'll be watching to make sure he treats you right."

She drew back and smiled up at him. "Thanks. That means more than you can know."

With that behind her, there was only one thing left to do.

Talk to Joe.

"I'LL HAVE ANOTHER," Joe said to Larry Goodman, the owner of the Courage Bay Bar and Grill. The place wasn't really open yet, but Larry allowed the emergency-services personnel to come in as early as they needed to.

Joe's gaze lingered on the banner across the far wall and the endless rows of photographs hanging there of those who'd given their lives in the line of duty. *Lest we forget their selfless acts of courage,* the banner read.

Larry poured Joe another cup of strong, fresh-brewed coffee. "You look a little down in the mouth this morning."

"Had a bad night," Joe admitted. He'd tossed and turned, unable to sleep. What if Lisa turned down his proposal? What if it was already too late for him to make things right?

Larry reached across the bar and slapped him on the shoulder. "You'll be all right, boy—you come from good stock. The Ripani boys always hold their own."

Though his brothers hadn't ventured into the field of firefighting, they were well known in the community as upstanding citizens. Darryl, the oldest of the Ripani clan, was a school principal. Bill, two years older than Joe, was in retail as their father had been. He traveled frequently, promoting the latest in software products for the company he'd created. Both had stable lives, unlike their younger sibling.

Bearing that in mind, Joe appreciated Larry's encouraging words. If Joe's brothers could do the marriage thing and make it work, so could Joe. Though the youngest, he would be the first to experience fatherhood.

And he intended to give it his best shot.

As if his troubled musings had somehow conjured her, Lisa appeared at the door of the restaurant. Larry went to let her in and she made her way to where Joe sat at the bar.

"I hope I'm not intruding," she said quietly.

Joe liked to come here in the mornings when it was quiet and no one else was around. He did a lot of thinking here. Lisa must have remembered that about him from their time together. He tried to mentally list all the things he'd learned about her, but could only come up with their amazing physical connection.

"Have a seat," he offered. "You want some coffee?" He cringed, belatedly wondering if coffee was okay for the baby.

She shook her head. "I'm fine. I just wanted to talk."

This didn't sound good. Was she going to tell him that she'd chosen Greg? Joe abruptly felt like the loser on *The Bachelorette*. Only this was far more important.

"I guess you made up your mind?" He couldn't blame her if she chose Greg over him. His mother had laid it out for him crystal clear: Joe had given Lisa absolutely no reason to believe that he was the right guy for the job of husband and father. Why should he expect her to jump at his proposal? He'd taken her for granted. Hadn't done the first thing to show he was reliable when it came to personal relationships.

He had no one to blame but himself.

"I did," she allowed. "It wasn't easy, but I had to think of the baby and what was best for her...or him."

Joe looked at her then. Really looked at her. She was just as beautiful as he'd thought she was the first time they met, only this time he looked beyond her outward appearance. She was a good woman, one who loved life and cared deeply about other people—and animals. She deserved a hell of a lot better than him.

"Look, before you say anything, I want you to know that I fully understand what you likely think of me." He slid off the bar stool and stood, since she didn't appear eager to sit down. "Everything you've concluded about me is probably true. Marriage was the furthest thing from my mind. And to be honest, I'd be lying if I said I was really ready to settle down now. I'm not." He shrugged. "I hadn't even thought about it. But there are extenuating circumstances now."

Her expression turned graver with every word he said. Damn it. He wasn't doing this right.

"Yes, I asked you to marry me because of the baby," he said, rushing on. "But the truth is I care about you.

We had something special. We can make this work, whatever the circumstances."

She closed her eyes as if she didn't want to hear the rest, but he had to say it all.

"I can be a good husband and father, if you'll just give me the chance. I want to provide the right kind of home for my kid…for you," he added, knowing deep in his gut that the words were true. "I know we can do this if we give it the old college try."

She held up her hand. "Just shut up, Ripani, before I change my mind."

For a guy who had a reputation for sweet-talking the ladies, Joe had pretty much gone overboard here, Lisa thought. If he said another word, she wasn't sure she could stand by her decision. She wanted to believe him, but she had a feeling that desperation had motivated that rambling monologue more than anything else.

"Does that mean you accept my proposal?" he asked cautiously.

Lisa drew in a mighty breath and let it go. "Yes. Though it may be the biggest mistake of my life, that's exactly what it means. I will marry you."

The kind of smile that Ripani was famous for spread across that handsome face. To her utter consternation, her heart lurched at the sight of it. She really was doomed here.

"The sooner the better, babe."

Before she could grasp his meaning, he pulled her into his arms and brought his mouth down on hers. Her hands went instantly to his chest…to resist, she told herself.

But there was no resisting Joe Ripani.

Those firm, warm lips nestled fully over hers and he thrust his possessive tongue into her mouth without the usual foreplay. He held her tightly against him, allowing her to feel the hardness of his body and the desire he felt at her nearness. Her breath evaporated in her lungs and she melted against him. She had no choice.

And that was the way of it with Joe Ripani.

All or nothing.

She could only pray, as her senses scattered in the wind like so much dust, that this was the beginning of having *all* of him.

CHAPTER EIGHT

LISA SOON REALIZED she was mistaken to think the only tough decision was behind her.

"Completely unacceptable!"

She held her breath while her mother stomped around the living room of Lisa's childhood home.

"Mom," Kate calmly explained, "there just isn't time for the whole church-wedding scene." She glanced at Lisa and shrugged helplessly.

"That's right," Lisa added, grateful for her sister's support. "Time is of the essence here. We don't want to drag this out."

Her mother shot her a look that said it all. Ruth Malloy was disappointed that her youngest had gotten herself pregnant before wedding bells had rung. Her old-fashioned sensibilities were seriously ruffled.

"I should say not," Ruth said, her tone blistering. "You might have thought of that before."

Lisa turned back to her sister in hopes of rescue.

"A wedding at the firehouse will be exciting," Kate insisted. "Think how jealous the ladies will be that your daughter not only nabbed Joe Ripani but managed a wedding at Jefferson Avenue Firehouse with the chief and the mayor in attendance."

Lisa had to give it to her sister—she'd gotten their mother's attention with that one. The ladies were the members of the Catholic Women's Auxiliary Club. Ruth Malloy was a longtime member and the current vice president.

Ruth pondered the idea a moment, her gaze narrowed speculatively.

Kate and Lisa exchanged hopeful looks.

At last Ruth said, "I suppose that could work." She looked from one daughter to the other, her expression still suspicious. "That is, if your father agrees."

Lisa breathed her first easy breath since she'd made the announcement. She wasn't worried about her father's blessing. Carl Malloy had always been a pushover when it came to his daughters. He might not be exactly pleased that Lisa had the cart before the horse, so to speak, but he would deal with it.

Now all she had to do was figure out the details.

SEVEN DAYS.

One hundred sixty-eight hours, or thereabouts.

It wasn't nearly enough time, but the day was here just the same.

His wedding day.

Joe swallowed hard and resisted the urge to wince.

It wasn't that marrying Lisa was a hardship, especially under the circumstances.

But there hadn't been nearly enough time to get used to the idea.

Last night had been his final night as a bachelor. The guys had given him a great party right here at the station. Lots of beer and pizza and jokes. Even a dancer. No one had shed a single garment, not even the dancer. The whole event had been nothing but good clean fun.

Chief Egan's presence had guaranteed that, which was fine by Joe. The dead last thing he needed was more trouble. He'd gotten himself in far too much already.

His conscience pinged him. He wasn't supposed to consider Lisa and the baby trouble. Hadn't his mother told him that repeatedly in the last seven days? Both his brothers were pissed at him for producing the first grandchild without even bothering with a wedding first.

Lisa's mother, as well as his own, had wanted a church wedding—different churches, of course. Lisa had sidelined that potentially explosive situation with a command decision that the wedding would be held in neutral territory. Unfortunately, the Courage Bay Country Club had been booked, along with any hotel big enough to host the event.

That left just one place on such short notice.

Jefferson Avenue Firehouse.

Joe loved the idea and so did his pals. He'd have to thank O'Shea eventually, when he got over being ticked at her for coming up with the idea and suggesting it to Lisa.

His squad had gone all out. The outdoor area was decorated so that no one would even notice the basketball hoop or the nearby parking area. O'Shea had borrowed truckloads of ferns and other potted plants, big and small, to camouflage whatever she considered unsightly. Tables for the reception afterward and hundreds of folding chairs, every single row decorated with white satin ribbons, filled the recreational space behind the firehouse. Candles, ribbons, balloons—the works. O'Shea hadn't missed a trick. Everything was perfect.

The mothers of the bride and groom had given their approval when they arrived half an hour ago. If anyone had possessed second thoughts about utilizing the firehouse, they had dissolved the moment the mothers arrived and expressed their delights.

Joe adjusted his bow tie and stared at his reflection in the locker-room mirror. He looked like a damn penguin, but it was the proper attire for the occasion.

In just ten minutes he would be taking sacred vows.

A local justice of the peace had agreed to do the honors, since neutral was the catchphrase of the day.

"Ready?"

Chief Dan Egan stepped into the locker room, a broad smile on his face. Joe didn't miss the hint of amusement in those blue eyes. The guy looked impressive as hell in his tux. Tall and athletic, even at forty-five.

"Ready as I'll ever be," Joe admitted, dragging his attention back to the business at hand.

"You'll be all right, Ripani." He gave Joe a fatherly clap on the back. "I appreciate your asking me to be your best man."

"I'm glad you could be here." Joe shrugged. "It means a lot."

Asking one brother over the other would have been

a damn fool thing to do, so Joe had done the next best thing: he'd asked the chief. He respected and admired Dan Egan. Joe couldn't think of anyone else he'd want to stand up with him today, unless, of course, his own father had been available.

"Let's get this show on the road," the chief said. He gestured to the door. "After you, Captain Ripani."

Joe couldn't keep the grin off his face as he made his way to where the justice of the peace waited. He was glad to see so many friendly faces, including arson investigator Sam Prophet. Sam had apparently been damn busy lately. Joe had scarcely seen him around, but he knew of the arson-related cases under investigation. That Sam had made time to come to the wedding meant something to Joe. Although he was as nervous as he'd ever been, this day was important. He wanted to share it with his friends.

John Forester, Shannon's fiancé, was there, as well as Shannon's brother Patrick, who was Courage Bay's mayor, and her brother Sean, a fellow firefighter, and his wife, Linda. Friends and family from both the Malloy tribe and the Ripani clan filled every single chair.

Joe's grin faltered just a little when he noted Greg Seaborn among the guests. As if he'd felt Joe's gaze on him, Greg looked up. For a single beat Joe barely repressed the urge to point directly at him and shout a victory cry. But he didn't have to say a word. He was the one about to marry Lisa, not Seaborn. Besides, if he did anything like that, it would only lend credence to Lisa's fears that Joe couldn't handle the whole marriage scene. He had every intention of showing her differently. So with that in mind, he smiled big and wide for Seaborn.

It was his wedding day—he could smile if he wanted to.

LISA TRIED HARD not to fidget.

She recited over and over every bone in the feline skeletal system. Then the canine one. Anything to keep her mind off the here and now.

What if the wedding was a mistake?

A part of her kept arguing that it wasn't real. A *fake*. But she couldn't think that way. This was the right thing. It had to be.

She'd had an entire week to have second thoughts, and not once had she been plagued with doubt as she was today. But then, she had been rather busy. Pulling a wedding together in one week was nearly impossible. And it would have been, if not for friends like Shannon.

Lisa smiled. Shannon looked amazing in her dress. Anyone who wondered whether or not there was a feminine form beneath that firefighter gear had only to look at her today. The silky fabric of the gown hugged her shapely curves, and the royal blue color looked great against her skin.

Lisa looked at her own reflection in the cheval mirror. The ankle-length, formfitting white gown she had chosen wasn't fussy and wasn't actually even a bridal gown, but it did flatter her figure. She studied her still-flat tummy and suddenly wondered if Joe would find her attractive when her belly rounded with child. Doubt plagued her. She huffed an impatient breath. Now wasn't the time to worry about that.

She glanced around the room and smiled. A makeshift bridal chamber had been put together in one of the bunk rooms, complete with this lovely antique mirror. Shannon had really outdone herself. Lisa owed her big time.

"They're ready for us," Shannon announced, as breathless as Lisa felt. She motioned for Lisa to join her at the door. "Spike gave me the cue that the wedding march is about to start."

God bless her mother, Lisa mused. Ruth had agreed to the arrangements without much of a fuss, except for the tape-recorded music. She had insisted that her friend Gladys play the piano for Lisa's big day. Shannon, ever resourceful, had managed to get a piano here. A keyboard would have been so much easier, but Gladys insisted that only a piano would do.

As Lisa and Shannon moved into the corridor outside the bunk room, the first notes of the wedding march filled the air.

This was it…no turning back.

Lisa's stomach did a little flip and she took a couple of deep breaths, grasping her bouquet tighter.

Even if Joe hadn't told her that he loved her…even if he hadn't really been in the market for a bride…this was the *only* right course of action.

She was nearly certain. Their marriage would be real…eventually.

Shannon moved through the rear exit of the building and onto the red carpet runner ahead of Lisa. The crowd rose and turned to view the bride as she made her appearance.

Lisa's heart surged and she smiled widely at the friends and family gathered to share this special moment with her.

"My dear."

She paused and took her father's arm. Carl patted her hand and gave her a loving and reassuring smile. "You're so beautiful." He kissed her cheek then, and it was all Lisa could do not to burst into tears.

How many times had her father held her when she'd fallen and scraped her knees, or when her feelings were hurt at school? He'd always been there for her, just as he was now, ready to escort her toward her new life. Would Joe be that kind of father to their child?

It wasn't until her father had led her all the way to the front that Lisa saw Joe. The picture he made took her breath away. He looked so handsome and so serious. She knew he must be every bit as nervous as she was.

She said one last silent prayer. *Please let this be the right thing.* And then she took the final step toward her soon-to-be husband.

By the time the justice of the peace invited the groom to kiss the bride, Lisa's knees felt ready to buckle beneath her. The ceremony had only taken minutes, but it felt as if everything in her life had changed.

Nothing would ever be the same.

In that seemingly endless second as Joe's lips descended toward hers, Lisa saw her future flash before her eyes.

A new beginning.

A new life thriving inside her.

And then his mouth settled on hers, and all thought ceased.

The crowd roared around them. Joe's buddies cheered him on, ensuring that the kiss would be one the audience would not soon forget.

When he drew back, he looked deeply into her eyes and murmured, "Lisa, I—"

Whatever he was going to say was lost as the fire alarm wailed.

Firefighters dressed in formal suits and tuxedos rushed inside. Before Lisa could catch her breath after that kiss, someone was calling Joe's name.

He squeezed Lisa's shoulders and said, "It must be a bad one. Gotta go." He gave her a quick peck on the cheek and added, "I'll be back."

And then he was gone. A flash of black and white, he rushed after the other members of his squad, including her maid of honor, Shannon O'Shea.

AS THE RECEPTION BEGAN, without the groom and a number of the guests, Lisa learned that the duty squad had called for backup on the fire in progress. There had been no way Joe or any of the others could have ignored the summons. She understood that. It was part of who they were and what they did. Lives were likely at stake. She pressed her hand to her abdomen and knew with complete certainty that she and this child would face moments like this many times. Somehow she had to learn to live with it.

Lisa managed to hang in until the final guests departed. Kate and her mother insisted they had cleanup under control and that Lisa should go home to wait for her groom. There was no need for her to stay.

She felt exhausted. And a little deserted…actually.

She shouldn't feel that way, Joe was only doing his job. But as their wedding day wound down, his sudden departure felt like desertion.

Sam Prophet had gone out on the call, as well. Lisa didn't know fire procedure well, but it did seem odd that an arson investigator would go to the scene of a fire before it was determined to be arson.

Seeing there was nothing for her to do here, Lisa finally made her exit. It wasn't exactly the wedding day she'd always imagined, but it was what it was.

As Lisa slipped away, she took one last look at her mother and father as they worked together with the catering staff to clear up the remains of the big event. She smiled, feeling a sense of balance for the first time in more than a week. Kate and her husband were busily stacking chairs, along with Joe's brothers and their wives. Lisa wondered if she and Joe would ever fit together so easily, or would this marriage remain a matter of convenience?

She thought of the tiny life growing inside her. Somehow she had to make it right…for the baby's sake.

A short while later, Lisa was safely ensconced in her tiny cottage near the Bay. She slid off the white gown that had served as her wedding dress and draped it carefully over a padded hanger, then placed it in her closet.

Her bedroom was filled with packed boxes, ready to be moved to Joe's house when he had the time to pick them up. He'd come for a few things this week, but there was still so much to be moved.

The cottage she leased might be small, but every nook and cranny was full of mementos and…stuff. It would take time to blend her belongings with Joe's. The lease wouldn't be up on her place until the end of the month, so she'd decided she might as well take her time. She and Joe had agreed that sharing Joe's house would be best. He'd bought it when he first became a firefighter twelve years ago, right after he'd returned to Courage Bay following a three-year stint in the military. He proudly boasted that the place was paid for now. Lisa had to give him credit for that. Most single guys wouldn't have worried about buying a home.

Maybe Joe was a little more reliable than she'd thought.

She tossed her slip across the end of the bed and studied her nearly nude body in the full-length mirror. It would be three or four months before the pregnancy would be obvious. Her tummy would round, a little at first, before blooming fully those last couple of months. She'd watched her sister go through this twice already, and hoped that her pregnancy was as easy as Kate's. Their mother claimed the same good fortune. If Lisa was lucky, the trend would prove to be genetic.

Turning from her reflection, she donned a pair of comfortable slacks and a pullover blouse. She couldn't help wondering how Joe was doing. Her stomach knotted at the idea of his going into such a dangerous situation. That was something she would never get used to. She could try, but she didn't hold out much hope.

She wandered into the living room and crawled onto the sofa. God, she was so tired. And she didn't want to think. Thinking would only lead to worrying about Joe. It would be this way every night. Every moment he spent on duty would be a time to worry. There had to be a way to distract herself. That much worry couldn't be good for the baby.

Maybe she could occupy her time after work with redecorating Joe's house. He had no actual design theme—heck, there wasn't even so much as a picture hanging on the wall, unless you counted a firemen's calendar. But the place had two bedrooms, two bathrooms and a nice living room and kitchen. It wasn't huge, but she could do a lot with the space. She might need to run her ideas past Joe, though. Technically, it was his house.

She was too tired just now to make any real plans. Later, after she'd had a good night's sleep…maybe then.

JOE DIDN'T BOTHER with a shower. As soon as the fire was under control, his squad insisted that he get home to his new bride. Joe hadn't argued.

Now, at half past nine at night, with soot on his face and the stench of smoke hanging on his clothes, he broke every speed limit in town getting home.

Only to find his house empty.

He unlocked the door and went inside just in case the dark windows only meant that Lisa had gone to bed early. But the place was deserted. He frowned. Why hadn't she come home after the reception?

Maybe she'd gone to her mother's or her sister's.

Then it hit him. She had gone home. To her home.

Ten minutes later Joe parked in Lisa's driveway behind her rental car. Her place was dark, as well.

He started to call her mother but decided he'd check out the situation first.

Though the lights were out, the front door was unlocked. He'd have to remind Lisa that leaving her door unlocked wasn't a good idea. Courage Bay had its share of break and enters.

In the living room, he switched on a table lamp, and the dim glow cast a golden pool over Lisa's sleeping form. Joe sat down on the closest chair and watched her for a time. She'd changed into comfortable clothes and stretched out like a cat. A smile tugged at the corners of his mouth. She was so beautiful. He tamped down the urge to reach out and touch her. She needed the rest. He'd picked up a book on pregnancy and had learned that in the early weeks extra rest was necessary.

He could hardly comprehend how small the life growing inside her was at this stage. He vaguely remembered studying sexual reproduction back in school but hadn't paid much attention.

He wondered how it felt to be pregnant. The very idea that Lisa's body was protecting and nurture another life seemed incredible to him. Like any other guy, he'd known how babies came into this world, but somehow it was different now. This was his baby. A part of him.

The idea scared the hell out of him for the most part. But on another level it totally awed him. He wondered if that was why he'd almost said *the* words to Lisa after he'd kissed her at the end of the ceremony. Maybe he'd just been caught up in the moment. What he felt for Lisa was desire…plain and simple. These unfamiliar feelings were probably related to the baby, or maybe he was still pumped from the wedding and then the fire.

He pushed to his feet. Might as well get something accomplished. Lisa probably wouldn't appreciate waking up and finding him staring at her like this.

As quietly as possible, he loaded up several boxes and transported them to his house—to their new home. He hoped Lisa would feel comfortable there. He wanted this to work. Wanted to make a good, happy home for their baby. The next eight months would pass in no time. He'd never been one to procrastinate, not about the important stuff, anyway. Getting their marriage off to a good start would be his first order of business.

Joe managed to make a second trip to his house with more boxes before Lisa awoke. While he was there, he showered and changed. No point in scaring her to death on their wedding night. When he finally returned to her cottage she had rounded up her bags, the ones containing the things she would need right away, and placed them by the door.

"I ordered a pizza," she announced with a smile that looked several degrees shy of the genuine article.

"Great." Pizza would work. Then he remembered that they'd had reservations at John Paul's, one of the best restaurants in town. "Damn." He popped his forehead with the heel of his hand. "I forgot all about our reservations."

"It's okay. I canceled them while I was still at the reception, since I didn't know how long you'd be at the fire."

"Thanks." So much for getting off to a good start. This night was supposed to be special. "Look," he said, taking her hand in his, "I'll make it up to you."

"It's okay. Really." She moved away from him and pretended to be preoccupied with her bags. "How did it go?" She glanced back. "Anyone hurt?"

Oh, jeez. It only took one look into those eyes to know she'd been worried about him. He hadn't even thought of that, but he should have. He'd known this would happen.

"No one was hurt." He raked a hand through his hair and struggled to find the right words. Why did talking to her suddenly seem so hard? They'd never had any trouble talking before. Okay, so they hadn't done much talking. He bit back a curse and tried again. "Look, I know this isn't easy, but it's what I do. I can't make any promises about these kinds of situations. There'll be a lot of nights like this."

"I know."

She wouldn't look at him now. Just kept opening those bags, checking the contents and reclosing them.

"Lisa." He snagged her arm when she would have walked past him. "I don't want this to be an issue. You knew who I was before—"

"Before I agreed to marry you?" she said, cutting him off. "*Before* I made a mistake and got pregnant?"

He released a heavy breath. What the hell did he say to that?

She pulled free of his hold. "It's not you I'm upset with, Joe. It's me."

That didn't make a hell of a lot of sense. Before he could ask for an explanation, she went on.

"You're right. I know who you are. It's me I don't understand. Why did I waste any energy worrying about you? This is what you do…who you are. Yes. Yes. Yes." She flung her arms heavenward. "I know. I just can't pretend it doesn't matter. Okay?"

He nodded, thankful that she'd said what was on her mind. Both his brothers had warned him that communication was a key factor in a good marriage. As long as she was talking to him, they were moving forward. It was when the talk stopped that he should worry. Okay. Maybe they were off to a better start than he'd realized.

The doorbell rang, announcing the pizza's arrival. Joe took the box, shoved a couple of bills at the guy and closed the door. This was his wedding night. He needed a little privacy.

The pizza was consumed in silence. The tension had slacked off, but he still sensed an uneasiness in Lisa. The only anxiety he felt at the moment was over how long it would be before he could take his new wife to bed. He'd scarcely thought of anything else for the past seven days. Sex with Lisa was fantastic. That part of their marriage wouldn't need any tweaking whatsoever.

He smiled. Being married definitely had its fringe benefits. His gaze swept over her yet again. He had no reservations at all about spending the next half century between the sheets with Lisa.

Lisa Ripani.

His wife.

His woman.

A stab of jealousy sliced into his gut at the thought that she would have to go to work at the clinic every day with Seaborn. Let the guy look at Lisa the wrong way just once and Joe would pound him.

She belonged to him now. She was his. The baby was his.

Lisa stood and began clearing the table. Joe wasted no time in coming to her aid. Another tidbit his brothers had given him. *Don't let her do all the work. Show that extra consideration and the wife would make it worth the effort in the sack.* Something else he intended to re-member.

It was a good thing he'd spent some time with the men in his family this past week and gotten a heads up on how to handle this whole marriage thing.

"Ready to go home?" he asked when the kitchen sparkled.

She looked startled at his question but quickly recov-ered. "Sure. Yes."

Damn but she was nervous. It wasn't as if they'd never been together before. He didn't quite understand her jumpiness—unless being pregnant somehow made the lovemaking experience different. She was acting as though the thought of going to his place filled her with dread.

Hmm. He'd have to take a peek at that book he'd

bought and see what he could find out about sex during pregnancy. Lisa might need extra cajoling or—he grinned—maybe she would need to be on top. He could deal with that.

Joe insisted on loading her bags himself. When he'd settled her into the passenger seat, bags stowed in the back, he drove the short journey to his place.

Home.

Their home.

He opened Lisa's door. "I'll come back for the bags," he told her as he walked her to the front door.

His bride.

His wife.

Had a nice ring to it.

He hoped being pregnant hadn't changed her ferocity as a lover. He was definitely looking forward to a long night of tangling with her, skin to skin.

"Wait." He pulled her back when she would have gone into the house ahead of him. "I want to do this right." He swept her off her feet and into his arms. She gasped. "The groom is supposed to carry the bride over the threshold."

Joe placed a tender kiss on her forehead before settling her back on her feet just inside the door. "I can't wait to hold you in my arms," he whispered before moving lower to kiss the tip of her nose and then her mouth.

God, she tasted good. Soft and sweet and so damn hot. The pleasant tang of tomato sauce mixed with the unique flavor of Lisa.

She pulled away. "Joe...wait."

He nipped at her bottom lip. "We don't have to wait, babe, it's legal now." His mouth sought hers but she moved away.

When the haze of lust lifted from his vision, he could see that she was shaking her head. "What's wrong?" Had he held her too tightly?

She threw up her hands stop-sign fashion when he would have moved closer to her. "I'm sorry. I can't do this."

"I don't get it. Are you sick or in pain?" Maybe it was all the excitement. Hadn't he read something about too much excitement in that damn book?

"I can't pretend this is real. It doesn't *feel* real." She shook her head adamantly. "This…I just can't do this."

She ran into the guest bedroom and slammed the door.

Joe stood there, completely puzzled.

What the hell had he done wrong?

He tromped back out to the truck for her bags. Women. He would never understand them.

As he stacked her bags on the floor inside his living room, an epiphany struck.

He wasn't having sex tonight.

Some wedding night.

CHAPTER NINE

EARLY SATURDAY MORNING, after a wedding night spent
in separate rooms, Joe and Lisa headed to a secluded
mountain retreat for their weekend honeymoon getaway.

The tension in the air was thick enough to cut with
a knife.

So far, wedded bliss was nothing like he'd imagined
it. His eyes burned from lack of sleep. He'd tossed and
turned most of the night.

Sure, he'd expected the novelty to wear off in time.
His brothers and his married buddies had warned him
about that inevitability. What he hadn't anticipated was
the complete absence of novelty.

He felt certain it wasn't supposed to be this way. So
what the hell had he done wrong?

He'd married Lisa, planned a romantic getaway and
even moved most of her stuff to his place. That should
account for something.

But apparently it didn't.

A part of him understood that in Lisa's view, his proposal had been made out of necessity. And it had. But
they were married now, end of subject. He, for one, in-

tended to make the best of it. And, to his way of thinking, that meant great sex…at least for a while. Losing
his bachelor status should come with at least one perk.

He'd checked his handy pregnancy guidebook and
there was no reason listed to prevent them from enjoying a satisfying sex life right until the end.

Maybe Lisa didn't know that.

Nah. It was a female thing. She needed to be wooed,
to hear all the right words—words he wasn't so sure
about. Joe knew what Lisa wanted to hear. But she
would tell right away if he wasn't being sincere.

He'd read that during pregnancy, especially the first
trimester, a woman's emotions ran the gamut of extreme highs and lows. In other words, her emotional
state would be volatile.

Worry hissed from him on a sigh.

He'd have to deal with that. Allowing her to be upset
wasn't a good thing. He'd read that, too.

Damn, marriage amounted to hard work. He flicked
a glance in Lisa's direction. He wondered if she felt the
same way.

She stared out the window of the truck, her expression never changing. Truth was…she looked miserable.

What else could he do to make her happy?

And why wasn't she putting forth any noticeable effort herself? A marriage was supposed to be a partnership? Fifty-fifty. It sure as hell didn't feel like a team
project just now. But then, he wasn't the one going
through all the physical and hormonal changes.

"Maybe we should just go back."

The sound of her voice after the long stretch of silence startled him almost as much as her words.

"Go back? Why would we go back?" He spared her another glance. Was she that miserable in his company? He'd thought there had been a mutual attraction between them. The sex had been great. Couldn't they build on that?

She shook her head, still not so much as looking his way. "This just doesn't feel right. Why waste your money? Just cancel the reservations and I can spend the weekend putting my stuff away."

He took a few seconds to evaluate the best course of action. Giving her what she wanted had been his aim from the moment he'd proposed, but this might turn out to be some kind of reverse-psychology thing. What if she really wanted him to take charge and make her enjoy this weekend?

"It's too late," he said. "The reservations are nonrefundable." He flexed a shoulder in a nonchalant shrug. "Might as well enjoy the place. Spike said it was great. He took his girlfriend there last fall."

She didn't respond for a moment, then finally relented. "I wouldn't want your money to go to waste."

He took that as a yes.

WHEN THEY AT LAST REACHED their destination, Lisa had to admit that she was impressed. The cottage was nestled in the foothills of the forested mountains that rose high above Courage Bay. The view overlooking the ocean and coastline took her breath away.

Inside another surprise awaited her. The place was incredible, like a little chunk of paradise. Wood floors stained in a warm mahogany, vaulted ceilings and massive windows through which light poured into the cozy rooms. In the bedroom, an antique queen-size bed was the focal point, along with a fireplace and French doors that opened onto a private deck.

The decor was absolutely charming. She couldn't believe that Joe would pick a place like this.

It was…romantic.

And the man didn't have a romantic bone in his body.

"It's great," she admitted, surprised. Joe had stood in the center of the room the whole time she looked around, clearly waiting for her reaction.

His broad shoulders sagged with relief at her announcement. It confused her—amazed her even—that he was trying so hard to please her. She'd be thrilled if she thought it was for the right reasons. But she feared Joe had just one goal in mind—resuming the physical relationship that had led to this marriage.

As usual, he just didn't get it.

Marriage was about a lot more than just sex.

She understood exactly what was going on here. Joe had married her, and given her and their child his name. He wanted to create a stable, happy environment for their child. Lisa wanted the same thing. But basing their marriage on a physical relationship wasn't the answer.

It wouldn't last. She understood that. Obviously Joe didn't. Yes, sex between them had been great. But she needed more. She needed Joe to love her.

At least he was trying to make this marriage work. She had to give him that. Still, she had to be strong. If they jumped back into a sexual relationship, it would be great short term, but Lisa wanted this marriage to last. She and Joe had to explore their feelings for each other on a nonsexual level, deepen their emotional commitment. If that didn't happen Lisa was afraid they would both live to regret it. Worse, they might become bitter, and then their child would suffer.

"I'm glad you like it." He managed a smile, but the voltage was only a fraction of the usual Ripani dazzler.

This was precisely what Lisa had feared. They were both going to end up miserable if they didn't proceed with caution. Couldn't he see that?

Maybe getting married had been a mistake.

"Joe...I..."

"Hungry?" He patted his flat abdomen. "I'm starved. The kitchen is supposed to be fully stocked. Let's check it out."

He ushered her to the kitchen before she could say more. Of course, broaching the subject of a divorce this soon might be a mistake, too. She should probably wait a few more days and see how things went.

As Joe checked out the cabinets and the fridge, a thought occurred to her. They'd been married only twenty-four hours; would a divorce even be necessary?

The point was moot, since Joe would never go for it. He'd staked his claim, the deed was done. No turning back. She had to try, for Joe and the baby. It was the right thing to do. Not that it was a hardship on Lisa's part.

She'd fallen for Joe from the beginning. But would he regret what they'd done once the reality of their marriage sank in?

A thousand conflicting emotions churned through Lisa. The very thought of making Joe as miserable as she felt at that moment made her almost physically ill.

The bottom line was this: She loved him.

Damn. She'd fallen in love with Joe the first time he'd kissed her while she'd been examining Salvage, the black Lab who'd become the firehouse mascot. And because she loved Joe, she did not want him to be unhappy.

She dredged up her courage and forced herself to think of her child's future. She had to try to make this marriage work. She could do that for the baby, couldn't she?

All she had to do was act as if everything were wonderful, play along with Joe's determination to make the best of the situation.

The words echoed hollowly inside her. She wanted the kind of loving relationship her parents shared. The kind her sister had with her husband.

Was that too much to ask?

No!

There had to be a way to turn this shotgun marriage into happily ever after.

Any other ending was unacceptable.

This child deserved the fairy tale. Lisa intended to see that he or she got it.

JOE WAS RELIEVED that night when Lisa acted more like her old self. She talked, laughed…and sat next to him on the deck as they watched the Pacific pound the coast far below.

He had to admit that Spike had been right. This place was the perfect setting for promoting romantic feelings. He felt pretty damn romantic himself right now. He'd even prepared dinner. Just spaghetti, bottled sauce and prepackaged garlic bread, but Lisa appeared overjoyed at his effort.

"Another glass?" he offered, reaching for the bottle of sparkling grape juice. He'd made sure that nonalcoholic beverages were available. Alcohol and pregnancy did not mix. Other than the occasional beer, he wasn't that much of a drinker, anyway. He preferred keeping his mind clear and his hand steady, even when off duty. He never knew when he would be needed for backup. Just like yesterday at his wedding.

Being a firefighter wasn't merely a job. It was a way of life. He would never let any of his fellow firefighters down.

"Thank you." Lisa held her fluted glass steady while he poured the pretend wine. "I'm impressed that you knew that alcohol was off limits for me."

He shrugged as if it was no big deal. "I like knowing what I'm up against."

From her odd expression he was pretty sure he'd stuck his foot in his mouth.

"I mean," he amended, "I want to take good care of you and that baby. I figured arming myself with knowledge was a big step in the right direction."

Relief went through him when his explanation

seemed to satisfy her. Of all the burning buildings he'd entered and the victims he'd saved, this had to be the toughest job he'd faced.

Of course, he wouldn't be saying that out loud in this lifetime, not in Lisa's presence, anyway.

"Good idea." She looked thoughtful for a moment. "Neither one of your brothers has children yet, do they?"

He shook his head. "I got my information from the *What to Expect When You're Expecting* book. I picked it up at the local bookstore. It seems to cover almost every aspect of pregnancy."

"Do you mind if I read it, too? When we get back, I mean."

A genuine smile tilted his lips. He'd finally done something right.

"Sure. I'll bring it home from the station house. I've been reading it on my downtime."

"I can buy another copy," she said quickly. "You might want to keep that one at work."

"No. That's okay. We can read it together."

Silence fell over them. Joe wanted to kiss her…to show her how strong his desire for her still was, but doing so might make them lose the little ground they seemed to have gained.

That blue gaze, full of questions, held on to his. "I'd like that," she said. "We should do everything related to the baby together."

He nodded his agreement.

"I have my first appointment with the obstetrician next Friday. Would you like to come along?"

Anticipation soared in Joe. "Definitely. What's his name?"

"He's new in Courage Bay," she explained. "Dr. Maynard Metcalf. Several of Kate's friends are using him and they think he's great."

Joe couldn't recall hearing of a new doctor in town, but then none of his friends had wives who were expecting, and Courage Bay was growing larger every day. Until recently he hadn't even considered what school district he lived in: now he wanted to know if it was the right one. Funny that he now seemed to judge everything in terms of what was best for his child. He could only imagine what it would be like once the baby was born.

"I think I'll indulge myself with a bath and some of those elegant bath oils I noticed." Lisa stood and stretched luxuriously. "I'm exhausted. Maybe I'll go to bed afterward."

As usual, the mere mention of anything even remotely related to sex and his male equipment stood at attention. He wished he could chalk it up to her soft, sensual voice, but all it took was an errant thought or word. He felt certain that her statement hadn't been an invitation, but his body didn't seem to understand that sad fact.

Staying semi-aroused and completely frustrated 24/7 couldn't possibly be beneficial to his mental health.

"Enjoy," he croaked as she floated into the house. The winter-white silk slacks and blouse she wore gave her an ethereal glow in the gathering darkness.

For several minutes after she'd disappeared into the

bedroom Joe sat there, trying to decide what he would do with himself. He heard the water running in the claw-footed tub. Could imagine Lisa shedding those filmy garments and stepping into the neck-deep water. The images tortured his mind and body, making him so hard he could scarcely draw a breath.

Finally, when he could bear the tension in his loins no longer, he stood and went in search of his duffel bag. He hadn't run today, or yesterday, either, for that matter. A long, hard pounding on one of nature's trails should relieve some of the stress.

Desperation surged anew as he heard Lisa's soft moans of pleasure as she apparently slid into the bathwater. The sounds skittered across every nerve ending in his body, and images flashed one after the other through his mind. Her slender body, toned arms and legs, nicely rounded breasts, heart-shaped bottom. All that silky hair would likely be stacked on top of her head, leaving her long neck easily accessible. How he would love to nibble that delectable skin…lave every square inch with his tongue.

It took all his strength to turn away from the bathroom door. He had to get out of here for a few minutes. Run as hard and fast as he could, then he would regain control.

Somehow, some way, they had to connect physically again.

He wanted her…cared for her. What did he have to do to prove it?

Joe headed down the trail that led from the chalet.

What else did she want?

The answer to that question, which deep down he already knew, haunted him for the next five miles.

LISA SIGHED as the warm water lapped around her chin. The heavenly scent of lavender sweetened the steamy air in the room. She loved the claw-footed tub…the sensual curves, the depth. Who needed a whirlpool tub when they had a treasure like this? The contours molded perfectly to her back, making this the most relaxing soak she'd ever experienced.

She imagined the elegant tub was a reproduction, since the original probably wasn't so ergonomically sensitive, but she greatly appreciated the aesthetics, as well as the comfort.

She fingered the delicate gold chain with its simple pearl resting against her throat. A wedding gift from her mother. Lisa had gasped in surprise when her mother fastened it around her neck. She recognized the lovely piece of jewelry as the one her grandmother had given to Ruth when she wed. Lisa hadn't expected her mother to part with it, but Ruth had insisted, saying that Kate had been married in Ruth's wedding dress, so it was only fair that Lisa get the necklace.

She had never been one to wear much jewelry, but she would truly cherish this piece.

Her gaze moved to her left hand and the simple gold wedding band there. There wasn't anything eye-catching about it. That Joe had gone to the trouble of picking it out himself made the ring quite special, however.

Shannon had told Lisa he'd gone to every jewelry store in Courage Bay until he found just the ring he wanted. What Shannon found amusing was that it looked like almost every other wedding band she'd ever seen. She, too, realized that Joe had taken the task very seriously.

Lisa couldn't help wondering if she would have the chance to cherish the ring the way she did the necklace her mother had given her. Would this ring come to stand for that level of commitment…for that much love?

She couldn't say just now. She wanted to give Joe and this marriage the benefit of the doubt. She only hoped that he would learn to love her the way that she loved him, and yet she was so very afraid to hope. What if she was in this alone? What if Joe never loved her like that?

Would the marriage and a perfunctory relationship be enough? Would their child notice his parents' marriage was a sham?

There was no way to know. Time would tell.

That's the last piece of advice her mother had given her before the wedding.

Trust your heart, dear. Time will tell.

She could do that. She was strong. Despite the moments of pure terror she experienced and the occasional certainty that she and Joe were doomed, Lisa had every intention of giving this marriage her all.

She thought of the child growing inside her and then of the man who'd planted that seed deep in her womb. He was a good man. Her eyes closed and her thoughts went instantly to the last time they'd made love. She wanted so very much to make love with him again. But she was scared that sex would muddy the new kind of bond they desperately needed to develop.

She had to be strong. The next time they made love, it had to be about love, not lust.

It wouldn't be easy, but it was for the best.

The water was cooling now, so Lisa pulled the plug. It was amazing how much more relaxed she felt as she stepped from the tub. She'd have to do that more often. As long as the water wasn't too hot, she'd read that baths were perfectly safe during pregnancy.

After drying off, she wrapped a fluffy towel around her body. All she had to do was brush her teeth and blow-dry her hair, then she planned to crawl between those satin sheets and sleep like the dead.

She stilled. There was only one bed. She wondered if Joe would mind taking the couch. Maybe they should have discussed that. Right now, though, she wanted to revel in the lingering afterglow of her luxurious soak.

After squeezing toothpaste on to her brush, Lisa scrubbed her pearly whites then spit into the basin. She twisted the cold-water tap but nothing happened. Where was the water?

She gave the hot a twist. Again, nothing happened.

Having survived several years of dormitory living and then low-rent apartment dwelling, Lisa had gained a respectable knowledge of how plumbing operated.

Since the tub faucet worked, there was no reason to suspect a problem with supply. This place was a rental. Maybe the owner had adjusted the valves to the off position when it was vacant and had forgotten to reset them in the vanity faucet.

Only one way to find out.

Lisa got down on her knees and opened the cabinet doors. She made a sound of dismay at the plumbing setup. She hadn't seen a maze like that in the worst of the dumps she'd rented during her college days. Who the hell did the plumbing around here? She could do better than that.

"Ah-ha," she murmured, finding the location of the valve. She reached deep into the back recesses of the vanity and attempted to twist the shutoff valve. Damn. It didn't want to budge.

She considered calling out for Joe, but, hey, she could do this. The last thing she wanted was for him to get the impression that she was helpless. Quite the contrary. Not once since she'd moved out on her own had she had to call in help for anything but wiring. She liked the challenge in doing her own repairs, and felt liberated by it.

Poking her head as far into the cabinet as she could, she positioned her arm for the utmost leverage and gave the valve another twist. The knob turned ever so slightly. Whoever had turned off the valve had tightened it too much.

Now for the hot-water side. Between the bizarre plumbing configuration and the confines of the small cabinet, Lisa could barely reach that side. Voilà! She found the valve and gave it a twist.

Smiling proudly, she started to back out of the cabinet, when her hair snagged on something.

"Ouch!"

Barely keeping her balance, she reached up with both hands to work her hair free.

The more she worked, the worse things got. She swore repeatedly as her hair seemed to tangle more and more with the pipe fittings. It wasn't until she realized the delicate gold chain of her necklace was involved that she really panicked.

She couldn't break that chain. It would kill her mother. And devastate Lisa.

This necklace stood for hope...hope for her marriage to Joe...for their child's future.

She couldn't break it now!

Lisa struggled to untangle her hair from the pipes until her arms ached from being in the awkward position too long. She just couldn't hold this position any longer. She sagged against the musty interior of the cabinet and admitted defeat.

She needed help.

"Joe!"

The silence pressed in on her. Why hadn't she noticed how quiet it was? Was he still outside? "Joe!"

Nothing.

She tried again without success to free herself, but her efforts seemed to make matters worse.

There was nothing she could do except wait for Joe to come inside.

JOE BOUNDED UP onto the deck, his lungs burning, his muscles throbbing with the workout.

Though he hadn't measured the distance, he was relatively sure he'd done seven or eight miles. But the additional exertion had worked like magic. He was spent. He didn't have enough energy to blink, much less work up a hard-on.

The cottage was quiet. Lisa was probably asleep by now. He would take the couch so as not to disturb her.

He went through a cool-down ritual on the deck before going inside. A couple of bottles of water followed by another sandwich and then maybe an ice-cold soda was in order. Then he would fall asleep on the couch.

"Joe!"

The weary sound of Lisa's voice put his senses on instant alert. He burst into the bedroom, found it empty and then rushed into the bathroom. He didn't bother knocking. The desperate, almost feeble cry kept echoing in his head. What if something had happened to the baby? He'd read that miscarriages often occurred in the early weeks of pregnancy.

His heart rocketed into his throat.

"What's wrong?"

It took three full seconds for his brain to analyze what his eyes saw. Lisa, clad in only a towel, kneeled half in and half out of the small vanity cabinet. She motioned with her hand for him to come to her aid.

"You have to help me," she wailed.

What the hell?

Confusion derailed rational thought and her shapely legs played havoc with Joe's relaxed state. He crouched down next to Lisa's nicely rounded bottom, which was the most prominent part visible.

"My hair and the necklace…the one my mother gave me…are tangled up in the plumbing. I'm afraid I'll break the chain if I pull too hard."

"O…kay," Joe said, dragging out the syllables. "How can I help?"

"Get in here and get me loose!"

There was nothing vulnerable about her tone this time.

Joe ducked his head inside the cabinet, which was as dark as pitch, their bodies blocking any possible light.

"I'll need to get my flashlight."

"Well, hurry!"

He double-timed it out to his truck and fumbled in the console until his fingers wrapped around the cold steel of his Maglite. He didn't take time to think, just rushed back into the bathroom.

If he thought about what he was doing, he might not survive the rescue. The temptation to take Lisa right there on the floor threatened his resolve to respect her wishes regarding their marriage. And he knew what her reaction would be to that.

He clicked on the light and moved back into position, his chest pressed against her back, his pelvis rubbing against her lush bottom. Ignoring the bombardment of sensations, he went to work. "Jeez," he muttered, "who plumbed this thing?"

"My guess would be a five-year-old kid who used a jungle gym for a model."

Joe chuckled softly. "That's a good guess."

With Lisa holding the flashlight, he slowly started to detangle her silky hair and the fragile gold chain.

"Why don't you tell me how you managed this unusual predicament?" he inquired in an attempt to help her relax. He could feel the tension vibrating through her.

"I was attempting to turn on the shutoff valves. The owner obviously forgot to do it." She huffed in frustration. "As you noticed, it's a jungle under here."

His smile widened. "You'll get no argument from me." That she even knew what a shutoff valve was, much less where it was located, gave him a sense of pride. His new bride was obviously pretty handy.

"I can't believe I did something so stupid," she muttered, disheartened.

"Hey, look at it this way," he suggested cheerfully, "it'll make a great tale to tell our grandchildren."

His fingers stilled when she remained oddly silent. Why was it that nothing he said was ever right? He continued with the task, telling himself that all newlywed couples likely went through this, though maybe not on the honeymoon. But everyone he'd talked to mentioned an adjustment period.

At last she was free. They eased out of the cabinet and collapsed against it. "Thank God." Lisa pushed the hair back from her face. "You're a lifesaver, Ripani. Not once but twice." She smiled unexpectedly and Joe's heart reacted.

Damn but she was beautiful when she smiled.

"It's my job," he murmured, wishing like hell he could slow the heat rushing through his body. Just touching her had him fighting to resist his baser urges.

He wanted to take her in his arms...wanted to kiss

her until she grew pliant beneath his assault. Then he would carry her to the bed and show her how much he wanted her…needed her.

As if she'd read his mind, she raised her fingers to her lips. Those heavy-lashed lids swept down over her eyes, banishing the desire he'd seen reflected there.

"Good night, Joe."

Before he could say a word, before he could tell her how glad he was that they'd come here, she was gone.

Joe sighed and hoisted himself to his feet. Fat lot of good that run had done him. He moved to the shower and turned on the water—the cold water.

This was just something else he'd have to get used to. Cold showers.

CHAPTER TEN

BY WEDNESDAY of the following week, Lisa felt "moved in" at Joe's place. All her worldly possessions were now under the same roof as his. As were the mound of wedding presents, still unopened. Her mother and Joe had stacked all the boxes in the second bedroom. She would get to those eventually, which also meant thank-you cards. In fact, she had a lot of thanking to do—to Shannon in particular.

Still, getting fully moved was a major accomplishment, which would not have been possible had she not taken a couple days off from the clinic. Greg had insisted the moment he saw her on Monday morning that she should go home. She imagined she must have looked beyond exhausted. Depressed, too.

It wasn't that she hadn't enjoyed the weekend retreat to some degree, but there had just been so darned much tension. She felt stressed to the max.

Nothing she'd attempted to do seemed to relieve it.

Thankfully, moving had helped. Greg had been right. Her life had been in such disarray that she'd needed the time to pull it all back together. The physical exertion had helped, as well as the mental closure of walking away from her small cottage and the past it represented.

With Joe on a double shift at the firehouse, meaning forty-eight hours, she'd scarcely seen him. She wondered if the extra shift had been necessary because someone was out sick or if he'd simply needed time away.

As much as she hated to admit it, she was grateful he was. Joe had probably needed a little distance, too. She'd sensed the continued tension, though she suspected that his came from a different source.

He couldn't stand that she wasn't prepared to enjoy a physical relationship. But she just couldn't go down that path yet. Why couldn't he understand that?

It just didn't feel right...

But as her mother so aptly put it, men did have needs. It wasn't fair for her to deprive Joe. They were married, after all.

Lisa lifted a skeptical eyebrow. Pardon her French, but *bullshit*. His needs weren't any greater than hers, and she wasn't about to sacrifice them for him.

Feeling empowered by her little "go Lisa!" rally, she headed into the living room to start hanging pictures. A house didn't feel like a home until photographs of relatives, dead or alive, were hanging on the walls.

When she'd finished with her own, she scrounged around until she found a few of Joe's family. Wedding photos of his brothers and their wives, and a great shot of his mother and father years ago.

Perfect.

Completion of the task required a trip to the local supercenter for more frames and picture hangers. Lisa deftly slipped her hair up into an old-fashioned knot and checked her jeans and T-shirt. She looked just like the gals on the craft shows on her favorite home decorating-channel.

She slid her feet into comfortable shoes and headed out. A quick mental checklist and she could be in and out of the store in twenty minutes. Today would be Joe's first day back home since they returned from the mountains. She wanted everything in place for him.

A smile lifted the corners of her mouth when she thought about the lovely family heirloom quilt she'd decided to use on their bed, and the lace curtains. It made the room almost as romantic as the one at the cottage they'd shared this weekend. She still needed to pick up bath mats for the two bathrooms, and linens more appropriate for the second bedroom.

Scratch that, she decided. That room would be the nursery.

An entire revamp would be necessary in there from paint to floor covering, curtains to light fixtures.

But would any of the changes make a difference? Would Joe notice? Would he realize that she was making his house their home? For them as well as their baby? She wanted desperately to form that kind of bond with him. To feel that they were making a new home together. But what if it didn't happen? What if the only level they could relate on was physical? Stop right there, she ordered. She wasn't about to let anything ruin her day. She'd taken this time off to pull her life with Joe together. A little optimism was in order.

She'd have to buy Greg lunch for insisting she take the time off. He'd been so right about it. Hadn't she read that pregnancy brought on the nesting instinct? Well, she was determined to make her nest as eye pleasing as it was functional. Joe had a nice home—*they* had a nice home, she amended—though it was a little drab.

Other than painting, there wasn't much she could do about the paneling in the living room. But a few splashes of color in the drapes and accessories would make a big difference. She mentally added those to her shopping list. Making a cozy home was the first step toward a more cohesive relationship, she hoped.

She glanced at the clock on the dash of her rental car—11:40. She might as well take Greg out to lunch today, if he was available. With so many of her appointments rescheduled to accommodate this time off, there was no telling when they'd have the opportunity again.

With speed dial she had Nancy on her cell phone in mere seconds. And Lisa was in luck, Greg was available and delighted at the invitation to have lunch with her. They agreed to meet in twenty minutes at the Courage Bay Bar and Grill.

The food was great and the atmosphere was relaxed. Perfect.

JOE PARKED in his driveway and frowned when he noted Lisa's rental car missing. Had she changed her mind and decided to go back to work today?

Damn. He'd volunteered for that extra shift to give them some space. But now he looked forward to spending some time with his wife. Maybe take her on a picnic at the beach. She liked picnics. She'd told him that before.

Instantly, the thought of being alone with Lisa was like a blast to his senses. He took a moment to get himself back under control before he got out of his vehicle. If by some chance she *was* home, he didn't want her to see him sexually aroused yet again. It seemed to be a perpetual condition when he was in her presence. Or, hell, whenever he just thought of her. So far as he could tell, she didn't appreciate his problem.

He didn't get that. Didn't she like the fact that she affected him? Why would she resent his physical desire for her? He had to find a way to figure out what he was doing wrong. So far, as a husband, he'd totally bombed.

Joe strolled up the walk to his front door and unlocked it. Stepping inside, he resisted the urge to shout, "Honey, I'm home." Not just yet. She might not appreciate that bit of humor.

His whole life now appeared to revolve around what Lisa would and wouldn't like. He tossed his keys onto the table. When was he supposed to get what he liked?

The word *never* flitted through his mind, but he squashed it like a bug. His time would come, that certainty was all that kept him sane.

The change in his living room wasn't noticeable until he did a double take. She'd hung pictures on the walls, and not just one or two. They were family photos. Her mother. Her father. Her sister and brother-in-law. Her niece and nephew. Her grandparents. He peered at the photo in question. He remembered meeting the elderly couple at the wedding.

On the coffee table he found a half dozen or so photographs of his family.

He shrugged. No problem. He didn't mind having pictures of his relatives around. There were worse things.

He trudged into the kitchen and opened the fridge. The bulb glaring back at him was about all it contained. Why hadn't Lisa gone shopping for food? She'd been at home for two days. Joe ate so many meals at the firehouse or at his mother's house that he didn't keep his own fridge stocked. But he thought Lisa would want to have groceries around.

Then he checked the cabinets.

Nada. Except for his own basic supplies.

Didn't the woman eat?

The book he'd been reading on pregnancy emphasized the importance of nutrition. Lisa was a smart lady. Surely she would know that and be watching her diet. Then he remembered the pizza she had ordered on their wedding night and the fact that he'd done all the cooking over the weekend.

Well, so much for eating a home-cooked meal with his wife today, or maybe any other. She might not even like to cook.

He'd have to talk to her about that. But he'd have to be careful. He didn't want to sound critical.

He scrubbed a hand over his stubbled chin. Man, he needed a shave.

Something in the corner of his eye snagged his attention. A dish towel on the counter. He picked it up and scrutinized it. Definitely not his. He didn't do flowers or ducks. He opened a few drawers and found more of the lively towels with matching oven mitts. Lisa had brought over her plates, too. As he peeked behind one cabinet door after the other, he found a full set of stoneware. Glossy white with bright flowers adorning the center. At least there were no ducks.

Tablecloths. Coordinating cookware. The whole works.

No problem. The kitchen was her domain, anyway. Well, it was supposed to be. He'd have to be careful not to judge her by his mother's standards. Women were different now. Lisa ran her own business. Maybe he should count on doing the shopping and cooking—or at least some of it.

He strode toward his—their—bedroom to see if she'd made any changes there. Might as well check the place out while he had a chance without Lisa there to see his reaction.

His eyes bulged when he halted in the doorway to the bedroom. "Holy cow," he muttered.

Gone was his nice plaid comforter, the down-filled one that he loved. And where the hell had those lacy things on the windows come from?

He walked to the closest window and touched the flimsy fabric. Good thing there was a pull-down shade behind them. The thin stuff wouldn't give any privacy whatsoever. And he had very private plans for the near future.

There were coordinating framed prints on the wall. More flowers. Well, he could live with them.

Might as well wash up while he was here. Maybe he'd shave. Spruce up a little before Lisa got home. Oh yeah. He'd tell her how great the house looked and win himself a few points.

Shoot. He had this game nailed. He knew all the right moves. Well, most of them anyway.

He opened the medicine cabinet and a shower of products spilled out.

"What the…?"

Prenatal vitamins. He'd read about those. Mascara. Tweezers. Aspirins, pills for bloating and PMS. Lisa wouldn't need those for a while. Various creams in tubes and bottles. Antiwrinkle cream that contained sunblock. Night cream. Undereye cream. Hair-removal cream. Something called concealer. He read the label on one or two of the other creams and his eyes widened in disbelief. Damn, there was some hefty upkeep to being a woman.

Joe shoved all the products back into the medicine cabinet and decided he was glad he was a man. All men did was wash and shave, for the most part. His wide grin faded as the realization that all of his stuff was missing sank fully into his brain.

Dropping into a crouch he surveyed the cabinet under the basin. Tampons, panty liners, hair gel, mousse, hair spray, hot rollers, curling iron, hair dryer. What the hell was she going to do? Open a beauty parlor?

Surely it didn't take all that stuff to keep a chick looking like a hot babe.

And what was up with all the tampons and stuff? That action wasn't supposed to be happening for the next few months. Thank God. His brothers and pals had warned him that women were not happy campers during that time of the month.

But none of this explained where his stuff was. He moved to the cabinet over the toilet and found the meager products that kept him fit for mingling with society. Shaving cream, a little aftershave, his razor and deodorant, toothbrush and toothpaste. He needed nothing else. Big deal if she'd exiled his stuff to the holding shelf over the john. He was a guy.

His stomach rumbled, diverting his thoughts from grooming products and decorating. Since it didn't look as if Lisa planned to come back anytime soon, he might as well go catch up with his buds at lunch. The squad had planned to rendezvous for lunch at their favorite haunt.

Sounded like a good plan to him.

Maybe Lisa would surprise him with a home-cooked meal tonight. She might be out shopping right now, planning a welcome-home dinner for her man. He could deal with that.

"YOU DON'T HAVE TO BUY my lunch," Greg insisted, a gentleman to the very end.

Lisa had made up her mind. She was going to find him a girlfriend and soon. Playing matchmaker might be fun. There were lots of women who would love to snag a great catch like Greg.

"Forget it." Lisa waved away his protest. "This is my treat." She turned to the waitress, "One bill only."

The waitress smiled and hurried away to place their order. The rooftop and dining room were filled to capacity, so they'd been relegated to a small table in the bar area. But Lisa didn't mind. She wasn't going to let anything get her down today. She'd even decided to go grocery shopping after lunch. She'd never been one to keep a stocked kitchen since she rarely bothered to cook at home, but things were different now. A wife was expected to prepare meals at least part of the time. Keeping the kitchen stocked would be just as much her responsibility as Joe's. There were so many things they needed to talk about, to work out.

"Now, tell me what's been going on at the clinic since last Friday."

Greg had closed the clinic at noon on Friday so that he and Nancy could attend her wedding. He'd been so sweet about that. She wouldn't have blamed him if he'd refused to come.

"Well, let's see." He considered her question for a moment. "Audra Hailey brought her cat in again. And once again I couldn't find a thing wrong with him."

Now, there was a good starting place. Audra Hailey had a huge crush on Greg. She was always bringing her cat in for some symptom that the animal only seemed to suffer in her presence.

Lisa nodded knowingly, though she doubted Greg had a clue what was behind Audra's visits.

"Oh, and we had another dog left on our doorstep."

Lisa had long ago put the word out that if anyone in Courage Bay decided they could no longer keep their pet and had no one else to take it, the animal was welcome at her clinic, even if space was limited.

"You know, Joe's house is pretty big and there's a fenced backyard. I can always bring the dogs home with me if need be." She'd only just now thought of that. Another reason to like her new home. A warm feeling spread through her as she thought of the man who went with the house, and she suddenly knew, without doubt, that things were going to work out for her and Joe.

"It may come to that," Greg admitted. "Space is getting rather tight around the clinic. Come summer, more people will be looking for pets, so it would likely only be temporary."

"Not a problem," Lisa assured him. "I've got plenty of space now." Her cottage had been tiny inside and out. The lease agreement wouldn't allow her to put up a fence in the minuscule backyard. But her new home was perfect.

The waitress delivered their drink orders and Lisa took a long draw from her lemon-garnished water. "Did the accountant finish up our taxes?" She'd delivered the last of the receipts to him the day of the earthquake. Surely he'd completed the final paperwork by now. His office hadn't suffered any damage from the quake, and the partnership forms were due in by March 15. But then, the accountant would know that.

"He delivered them today," Greg told her. "You could stop by and sign them on your way home. Or you can wait until you come back into the clinic tomorrow." He fiddled with his glass and cleared his throat. "You are coming back, aren't you?"

His question surprised her. "Of course I am. Whatever gave you the idea I might not?"

The uncertainty in his eyes surprised her.

"With the wedding and the baby, I thought maybe you might not have as much time as you've had in the past," he explained.

He was hedging. What in the world had given him such a ludicrous idea? "Greg, don't even think it. I'll be back tomorrow. It's true I might have to take off more time than before, and I might even cut back from ten hours a day to eight, but I'm fully dedicated to our clinic."

Greg nodded his approval and obvious relief. "Good. I wouldn't want to lose you." He sighed, then admitted, "I guess I was just worried that Joe wouldn't want you working with me at the clinic considering I asked you to marry me, and all."

"Don't lose a minute worrying about Joe." She patted Greg's hand. "He knows how much that clinic means to me. He doesn't have any problem with us working together. We're friends and he understands that."

SPIKE'S WORDS HALTED midsentence and he stalled just inside the front entrance to the Bar and Grill.

"What?" Joe prodded him. "You didn't tell me what happened after that?" He hated when someone started a story and then didn't finish it.

What the hell was wrong with the guys? Spike, Bull and the rest of them just stood there, half in and half out of Larry's place, their gazes riveted on something Joe couldn't see.

"Is there a fight?" That was Joe's first thought. But when he pushed through his fellow firefighters, he found that it wasn't a fight, but the sight of his new wife having lunch with the man who had proposed to her before Joe that had stopped them in their tracks.

The man Lisa had said yes to before Joe talked her out of it. And she was touching his hand!

Seaborn.

The snake.

Joe wouldn't have thought the guy would stoop this low.

Fury roared through him. He clenched his fingers into tight fists and an odd red mist swam before his eyes.

Seaborn was a dead man.

It wasn't until Joe had stormed halfway across the room that his buddies came back to life.

"Whoa, Cap'n." Bull was the first one to reach him. "You don't want to do this."

"Oh, yes, I do." Joe shook him off and covered the rest of the distance in four long strides. Lisa looked up at him just as he closed in on the table.

"Joe, you're—"

"I stopped by the house but you weren't home," he growled. He flicked a gaze in Seaborn's direction. The weasel at least had the good sense to look contrite.

"No," she said with a smile, seemingly oblivious to

his emotional state. "I was going shopping and I decided to have lunch with Greg to—"

"Let's go," he snapped, determined not to make a public spectacle.

"What?" The realization that he was mad as hell suddenly dawned in Lisa's eyes.

"You're coming with me," he growled.

"Excuse me," she said tersely. "I'm having lunch. You're welcome to join us, but if you think I'm leaving just because you say so, you can forget it."

"Lisa, it's okay," Greg urged. "We can do this later."

Lisa looked from her knuckleheaded husband to Greg, who appeared immensely uncomfortable.

What was Joe going on about? Lisa wondered, ordering her around like this. And in front of Greg.

How dare Joe come in here and act like a jealous ass! She would not tolerate that sort of barbaric behavior.

"No," she protested. "We're having lunch. Our food hasn't even arrived. He can just get over himself."

"Lisa, don't argue with him. It's all right—"

"Let's go." Joe's command was a snarl now.

Lisa couldn't remember ever being this angry. She wanted to…to kick him. What the hell did he think he was doing?

"No," she repeated in the same stubborn tone he'd used.

Some of Joe's firefighter friends had gathered around him now and were trying to calm him down. Lisa's head had started to spin a little. This was ridiculous.

When Joe reached for her hand, Greg stopped him,

the move startling Lisa along with everyone else around them.

"She said no, Ripani," Greg reminded Joe hotly. "There's no need for this sort of behavior."

Joe shook off his hand. "You're right, Seaborn. This is between you and me. Why don't we take it outside?"

"What's going on over here?"

Larry, the owner, pushed through the small crowd gathered around Lisa and Greg's table. Lisa's humiliation was complete now. She would never forgive Joe for this.

"Everything's cool," one of Joe's friends insisted.

Lisa had a feeling things were about to get worse.

"Ripani," Larry said, "I don't know what your beef is, but this isn't like you." He shook his finger in Joe's face. "You cool off."

Without a word, Joe stormed out the door, his entourage following.

Lisa knew a moment's relief. "Thank God. I don't know what got into him. He's lost his mind!"

Greg stood. "I'm sorry, Lisa, but we have to straighten out this matter in the only way a man like Ripani understands."

Before she could argue, he'd rushed out the door, as well.

"Oh, for the love of Mike," she muttered, before pushing to her feet and following the rest of the idiots out the door.

Joe had waited for this moment for two weeks. Anticipation surged through him as Seaborn faced him in the parking lot. They would settle this here and now.

Seaborn walked right up to him and looked him in the eye. Damn. The guy had a set of balls, after all. "I let you take her away from me," he said for Joe's ears only. "But you won't take my pride. I'm not afraid of big bad Joe Ripani."

Rage exploded in Joe's gut. This guy was going to regret the day he was born.

"I didn't want it to come to this," Joe said, which was pretty much a lie. "But you're not going to flirt with her anymore. She's my wife, Seaborn. Get that through your head."

"Stop this right now!"

Lisa forced her way between them. "Stop it!" she repeated. "This is ridiculous! Do you know how childish you look? Both of you?" She glared from Joe to Greg and back, hearing muttered agreement from their audience.

"You'd better listen to her," Spike called out. "You have to live with her, Cap'n."

Lisa cut him a look that shut him up pronto.

"He had no business bringing you to lunch," Joe accused. "I know what he's trying to do."

Before Greg could argue the point, Lisa blasted Joe with a comeback of her own. "I brought *him* to lunch, you big oaf!"

With that, she gave them both her back and stormed off, leaving Joe grappling with her words. *Lisa* had invited Seaborn out for lunch?

He never saw the punch coming.

Seaborn gave him a right hook that knocked Joe completely off his feet. He slammed into the ground like a fallen oak.

Joe blinked to clear his double vision. His head spun just a little. What the hell?

The next thing he knew, Lisa was hovering over him, demanding to know if he was all right.

When the world had stopped moving, he pushed himself up onto his elbows just in time to see Lisa shoot Seaborn an icy glare and then direct that same frigid look at him.

"Men!" she shouted. "You're all the same!"

And with that profound statement, she left.

Well, Joe thought, he'd done a bang-up job of winning her over.

At this rate, he wasn't ever going to sleep under the same covers with her.

Much less make her happy.

CHAPTER ELEVEN

HE'D ROYALLY SCREWED UP this time.

Lisa hadn't even spoken to him last night. She'd been so furious that she'd gone into the bedroom, slammed the door and hadn't come out until time to go to work.

God, he was a complete idiot. What had he been thinking, going off like that about Seaborn?

That was the trouble. He hadn't been thinking.

The Iceman never lost control.

The truth was, he rarely did any thinking where Lisa was concerned. He couldn't form a rational thought in her presence. He…cared too much. Wanted her too badly.

But how did he explain that to her?

She'd gone back to the clinic this morning, leaving him alone at home. It was only Thursday, not even a week of wedded bliss, and so far it had almost killed him.

What the hell? He emerged from his truck and headed into the station house. Most of the problems were his fault. He admitted it. He didn't have a clue how to make this work. All the advice in the world didn't appear to help. And he'd had about all the four-quiet-walls at home he could take. He could kill some time with the guys on duty today.

At least he could relax tonight. Thursday was his poker night and it was Joe's turn to host the gathering. Last week's game had been preempted by his bachelor party.

Inside the firehouse, he took the ribbing in stride. Seaborn had left him with a hell of a shiner—but only because Lisa had distracted him.

He had to admit, though, that kind of behavior wasn't like him. He didn't go around picking fights. But he'd be damned if he would apologize to Seaborn, even if he owed the guy one.

He moseyed into maintenance to check on one of the trucks his squad used. It was in for a tune-up today. Bud Patchett, the mechanic who maintained the vehicles, was the best. His motto was simple: Take care of the trucks and they take care of you.

"Hey, Bud, how's she doing?"

The mechanic looked up from his work and chuckled. "Better than you are, I hear."

Bud was ten or so years older than Joe, balding, with black eyes and the muscular shoulders and arms that went with his occupation.

Joe rubbed his tender jaw. "I could have taken him."

"I haven't got a doubt about that," Bud said as he turned back to changing the spark plugs. "It's taking care of your new missus that worries me."

Damn. Nothing stayed private around the station. "That so?"

"I just got one piece of advice for you, Cappie," the friendly mechanic went on. "Treat your lady the way she likes, and life will be a lot easier."

Joe thanked him and went off in search of another, less personal distraction. Unfortunately, Bud's sage advice had come a little late. Joe had already learned that lesson the hard way.

He had himself a plan in place. In fact, he'd already started. Hell, he'd cooked every meal they hadn't ordered out. He'd learned to operate the dishwasher and do laundry. What else did she want? Well, he knew there was more, and he was working on that. But tonight…well, tonight was his. He'd given up a lot for this marriage. One night, three measly hours, each week wouldn't hurt.

He would have reminded Lisa of the weekly ritual this morning had she been speaking to him. But she hadn't been. Not speaking, not having sex, nothing.

Lisa had always worked long hours at the clinic back when they dated. After several days off, she'd probably be working late tonight anyway. And if she did come home, she could just read in their room.

Poker night was sacred.

LISA FINISHED UP with her last patient about seven. She hadn't meant to stay past five, but there had been a run of emergencies.

By unspoken mutual agreement, she and Greg had not discussed yesterday's fiasco. She was almost as angry with him as she was with Joe.

And yet, she'd lain in bed last night and had to fight the nearly overwhelming urge to march into the living room, where Joe slept on the couch, rip off his clothes and join his hard body to hers.

Living under the same roof with him and not having sex was driving her crazy. Maybe she was wrong to banish that part of their relationship.

Joe might never be in love with her. Lust just might have to be enough. This marriage might be as real as it would ever be.

But, God, she wanted more.

Was she being selfish? Was she subconsciously torturing Joe in the one way she knew would get to him more than anything else?

Maybe.

Disgusted with herself, she closed up the clinic for the night. Greg had already called it a day. He hadn't wanted to. He'd wanted to stay until she finished, but she had ordered him to go.

Reluctantly he'd obeyed.

She had to find him a girlfriend.

If she did, maybe then Joe wouldn't be so tense about Greg and her working together, which was, in her opinion, the absolutely stupidest thing she'd ever heard. Her fingers stilled on the light switch. Was it? Would she be so quick to forgive if the tables were turned? What if Shannon had been in love with Joe for ages and had asked him to marry her? And this pregnancy had been all that had prevented Joe from doing just that? Would Lisa be able to accept their working relationship as nothing to worry about?

She had to laugh. Shannon and Joe would kill each other before they would succumb to any sort of attraction. They respected each other professionally and were

friends. Or at least they had been until the breakup between Joe and Lisa. Their personal relationship had
been a bit strained since then. Shannon was too pushy
for Joe's liking. Joe preferred to be in charge. He liked
playing the big bad protector. And Shannon already had
that part covered herself. Besides, Shannon had found
the love of her life, and John Forester was happy to let
her be the woman she was.

Maybe all Lisa needed to do was let Joe be the man
he was.

The man she'd fallen in love with before there was
even a pregnancy to consider. Joe was so strong…so
handsome…so utterly male.

The full clarity of what she'd done hit her then. She
had been punishing him. She loved him, there was no
doubt. Loved him just as he was. But the part of her that
needed assurances wanted him to commit to her the
way she had in her heart to him. Was he even capable
of that level of commitment? Not just Joe, but men like
him? Those who were brave enough to head into rag-
ing fires to save lives?

Would she have fallen in love with him had he been
more the way she wanted him now? She'd certainly
never fallen for Greg, who epitomized all those virtues.
Wasn't it the dangerous air about Joe that had attracted
her? The edgy, physical male?

She'd be lying if she didn't admit that was true. She
was the one being unfair. Joe was exactly the man she
had fallen in love with, but she had let him walk away
from their relationship—had pushed him, actually—

because he wouldn't change. Why was it women always fell for men and then tried to change them?

She knew Joe. Whether or not he ever told her he loved her, he would always be faithful to her. And a good provider. Why did her expectations of who he should be override the man he was?

"Good Lord, Lisa, you've been an evil bitch," she admitted aloud. She wasn't going to mold Joe to suit her idea of what a husband should be like. Joe's personality was far too strong for that. She would only make him bitter and unhappy.

She'd been wrong. She could see that now.

Though apologizing was out of the question, Lisa could mend her ways, alter her course. A plan started to form. Oh, yes. She could get things back on the right path. It would be simple. All it took was a little compromise.

Why hadn't she realized this sooner?

Shell shock, that's why. She'd suffered a near-death experience, then found out she was pregnant by the man who'd broken up with her weeks before. Then the whirlwind marriage. No wonder she'd been making Joe's life a living hell. She'd been grappling for her own emotional purchase.

Things would be different from now on.

She would carefully redirect the course of their fledgling relationship. It was almost too easy. She couldn't expect Joe to be the only one who compromised. As important as her need to bond on other levels, he needed the physical connection. Give-and-take, that was the answer.

"I CAN'T BELIEVE she let you host poker night," Bull said as he perused his hand. "Hit me again," he said to Spike, who was dealing this round.

"Hey, this is my night," Joe said with complete confidence.

"I figured after yesterday, you'd be in the doghouse for at least a month," Bull remarked.

Joe tapped the tip of his cigar on the ashtray. "I don't have a doghouse." He grinned and hitched his thumb toward the kitchen. "Anybody ready to chow down? I've got hot wings, ribs, the works in there. Picked 'em up at Larry's right before you guys got here."

Rumbles of "later" rose from the table. Bull, Spike and Gary, better known as Chug, were studying their hands, planning their strategy. No one wanted to think about food right now. Equal amounts of red, white and blue chips were stacked in front of each player. But that wouldn't last long. Joe intended to win every round tonight. He could feel Lady Luck sitting on his shoulder at that very moment.

This was his night.

Chug took a long draw from his cigar and blew out a puff of smoke. "Lemme have two."

Spike threw down two new cards and shuffled the two Chug had tossed aside back into the deck.

"So," Chug asked then, "what's it like?"

The whole table fell quiet, and all gazes shifted to Joe. He wanted to reach across the table and shake the guy. They weren't supposed to be talking about the M word. This was poker night. Women and relationships and all that jazz were forbidden.

"He doesn't want to talk about it," Spike said with a smirk. "Can't you tell it's pure h-e-l-l? I've never seen the guy so off-kilter."

Joe scowled. What the hell did Spike mean by *off-kilter?* "It's great," he snapped. "Everything's great. I just had to show her where I draw the line, that's all."

He couldn't miss their smirks, and Joe shot each of his pals a dirty look. "What? You don't believe me?"

"Damn, man," Bull said with a laugh. "She had you so off balance that you let Seaborn put you down." He leaned forward with a knowing expression. "Now, *that's* off-kilter."

"I was just worried about her being upset," Joe argued. "With the baby and all, emotional outbursts are not a good thing."

"I think you've been spending too much time with your nose in that book," Bull cautioned. "You're letting the important issues fall by the wayside."

If a single one of them brought up sex, Joe just might have to kill him.

"Not that we're trying to get in your business," Spike added. "But we have been concerned that perhaps there's a bigger reason for your being on edge all the time."

"Don't even think about it," Joe warned, murder in his tone.

Everyone but Joe burst into laughter. Joe clenched his jaw and grabbed a couple of chips to toss into the center of the table. "Let's get down to business here," he growled. "I've just laid down the first wager. Who's next?"

By seven-thirty Joe was kicking butts and taking names. No one was laughing now. These guys were in to him for some serious chores. At this rate, he wouldn't have to cut his grass all summer. Taking his turn cooking for the squad wasn't going to happen for a long, long time.

"I'm out!" Bull threw down his cards.

Spike and Chug exchanged cautious looks.

Joe just grinned, letting them think what they would. His hand this round actually stunk, but he had no intention of letting anyone in on that little secret. There was still an hour and a half to play. Things could go downhill fast and he didn't want to end up washing Spike's SUV every Saturday morning.

"When are you two going back up to the mountains again?" Spike asked.

Joe saw the question for what it was—an attempt to break his concentration.

"Maybe never," he said flippantly. "We've got the perfect little place right here. We don't need to pay for the ambience."

"I'm done." Chug surrendered his cards in defeat.

Now it was just Joe and Spike.

All Joe had to do was keep his edge for a few more minutes.

"Why don't we make this a little more interesting," Joe suggested. He pushed every chip he had but two into the stack in the center of the table. "Care to match that?"

Any second now, his good buddy would fold.

Spike's gaze narrowed suspiciously. "Why not?" He shoved all his chips forward. "Call."

A twinge of panic went through Joe. He'd been sure that tactic would work. Now he had no choice but to show his pitiful cards. Spike had called his bluff.

The front door opened and Lisa walked in. All four players looked up from the card table.

"Hey," Joe said, his voice giving away his trepidation. Damn, he hated when that happened.

She was home early. The thought that he should have called her at the clinic today and warned her about the game whizzed through his mind. She could have made other plans for herself.

Too late for that now.

Lisa looked from one cigar-puffing, beer-swilling firefighter to the next. Her mouth dropped open in something between disgust and surprise.

Joe knew this called for damage control.

"It's poker night," he said, pushing up from his chair and rushing to take the shopping bag from her arms. "Every Thursday night—don't you remember?"

He'd had poker night back when they were dating. Lisa must have forgotten. Why hadn't he reminded her?

Lisa opened her mouth to say something, but a sudden coughing jag cut her off.

The smoke, Joe realized. The smoke was making Lisa cough. *Shit.* He shot the guys at the table a look and cigars were instantly extinguished. He thought of the fact that she couldn't drink alcohol and he felt like a total jerk about the beer.

"Looks like this one's mine," Spike announced. He pulled the pile of chips toward him. "That makes it a night."

Joe didn't take time to utter the pithy comeback that remark deserved. But calling it a night was probably a good idea, judging by Lisa's reaction.

"You're right," Bull chimed in. He and Chug jumped up and started clearing the table.

When Lisa had caught her breath, she just stared at the guys scrambling to clean up the mess. She turned to Joe then and said the words that struck terror in his heart: "I'll spend the night at Mother's."

She walked out.

He couldn't believe it.

No matter what he did, it was never right.

"You'd better go after her, man," Spike warned. "Going home to Mother is bad."

"We'll clean up here," Bull assured him. "Go on."

Chug just shook his head.

Joe tossed the shopping bag aside and rushed out the door to catch up with his wife. "Lisa, wait!"

She hesitated at her car door and glared at him. The streetlight provided enough illumination for him to see that she was outraged.

"How could you do this, Joe?"

What the hell was the big deal? It was just a game of poker. Couldn't he at least have that? And why the hell did it suddenly sound so selfish?

"What's the problem? It's just a harmless game of poker."

Lisa couldn't believe that he didn't get it.

"The poker and your friends aren't the problem. The house is full of cigar smoke. Secondhand smoke is bad for the baby. Or did you skip that section of your reading?"

She wanted to scream. What was wrong with him? Just as soon as she convinced herself that she was the one making all the mistakes, he went and did something totally insensitive.

From his defeated expression, she knew that he'd gotten the point. "I'm…sorry. I didn't think."

"That's your problem, Joe," she ranted, on a roll now. "You don't get any of this."

She rummaged to find her keys at the bottom of her purse. She had to get out of here. She refused to let him see her cry. And the tears were burning like fire in the back of her eyes. She'd lost complete control. Confusion had her emotions running amok. Her plans for the night had been sidelined by the first bump in the road. Why couldn't she do this? It should be easy.

"You can't think I did this on purpose," he said softly. "I made a mistake. Don't you ever make any?"

Lisa closed her eyes and tried to slow the emotions churning inside her. "Yes."

"Do you really think I would do anything to hurt you or the baby?"

She didn't want to feel his nearness right now. Didn't want him to affect her the way he always did. Why couldn't they connect like this on any other level?

"No," she admitted. "I know you wouldn't purposely do that."

"Then why are you making me feel that way?" He fell silent a moment before continuing. "I can't do anything right. I'm at a complete loss here. Just tell me what to do and I'll do it. I want this to work, Lisa. I want it every bit as much as you do."

Before she could answer, Joe's buddies poured out the front door and hurried to their respective vehicles. Good-nights were exchanged and then they were gone, leaving Lisa with no other distractions to hide behind. It was the moment of truth.

"I know you want this to work, Joe," she said, letting him off the hook. "It's just that I'm not sure we're focused on the same goal. I need the emotional commitment, as well as the physical one."

Joe blinked. "I want that, too."

"Do you?" She looked up at him, searched his eyes for the uncertainty she knew she would find there. "Are you sure about that?"

"Yes. I'll do whatever it takes to make it happen."

He spoke without the slightest hesitancy. Maybe he was serious. Lisa had been pondering an idea all afternoon. She had a feeling it might be the fastest way of resolving the issues between them.

"All right," she said, "if you're really serious, then we need professional help."

An alarm went off inside him. One as loud and steady and reliable as the one that sent him roaring out of the firehouse whenever disaster occurred. He didn't have to say a word. Lisa saw it in his eyes.

"What kind of professional help?"

"We need to see a marriage counselor."

When he would have protested, she cut him off. "It's the only way, Joe. We're sinking fast. Will you do this?"

He'd told her he would do whatever it took. In the three seconds that elapsed before he answered, Lisa feared that he wouldn't back up the words.

But she should have known better.

Responsible was Joe's middle name.

"Anything it takes, Lisa. Just name the time and place."

LISA WAITED outside while Joe raised every window in the house and turned on the central fan. He finished clearing away the signs of his ill-fated poker game and fished a couple of bottles of water from the shopping bag she had brought home with her.

He watched her a moment before joining her on the stoop. She looked tired and kind of lost. Why was it that he couldn't make her smile like before? There had to be a way to do this. Somehow they had to hit their stride.

This constant charging from one extreme to another was tearing them apart.

"It won't take long for the house to clear out," he assured her as he sat down on the top step next to her. He passed her a bottle of water and opened the other one for himself. "The breeze will help." He inhaled deeply of the salty ocean air. He hoped like hell Lisa would say something, because he was drowning here.

"I didn't mean to ruin your game." She released a heavy breath of her own. "Tell your friends I'm sorry.

I just…" She shook her head in disgust. "I don't know why I got so upset."

"I do," he argued. "You were right. We'll dispense with the cigars next time. It was a stupid oversight."

She nodded. "They're bad for you, anyway." She took a swallow of the lukewarm water.

Joe licked his lips as he watched her throat work delicately. He wanted to taste her again…to touch every part of her. Slow down, he warned. Reaching that goal might just be impossible, but he had to at least try to keep things amiable. Inspiration struck. "You know what we should do?"

She turned toward him, clearly skeptical of what he might have in mind. Or maybe just desperate…like him.

"We should open those wedding gifts."

The ghost of a smile raised his spirits. "You're right—we should," she agreed with more enthusiasm than he'd hoped for.

Later, when the stench of smoke had cleared, they settled on the floor of the guest room and surveyed the pile of gifts.

"This looks almost too pretty to open," Lisa said of the first box she picked up, which was wrapped in silver paper and a white satin bow.

Joe reached for another. He leaned close to her as he did. "Just pretend you're still a kid and it's Christmas." He ripped off the bow and the paper, tossing it aside. "And there we have it," he announced as he held up a shiny black toaster. "The perfect gift."

Lisa laughed and tore open her own box. "Wow! A

crystal vase." She moved it so the light glinted off the intricate details.

"I'll bet I can top that." Joe snagged a glittering gold package. It was larger than the first two they'd opened. It had to be hiding something even better.

A platter. White stoneware.

"Oh, that's lovely," Lisa remarked. "That'll be perfect for Thanksgiving turkey."

They opened every single gift that way, until they were surrounded by mounds of wrapping paper and bows and dozens of elegantly decorated gift bags. Lisa had remembered they needed to make a list of names for the thank-you cards. Good thing, because Joe knew nothing about gift etiquette.

"I think we made a pretty good haul," he concluded as he surveyed the mountain of china, linens and small appliances.

"Very good," she agreed.

It was late. They both needed some sleep. "I guess we have to clean up now," he suggested with a serious lack of zeal.

They stood motionless for a bit, staring at the mess before Lisa responded, "Guess so. I'll get some garbage bags."

She made a move to go, but he captured her hand before she could get away. "I meant what I said tonight."

She held his gaze for a second that lapsed into ten and lacked the usual strain. "I know you do, Joe. We're both trying. As confusing and crazy as it's been, I think we're making progress." She smiled, her lips trembling a little. "Even if it seems like I'm fighting you, please know that I do want this marriage to work."

With that, she stood on tiptoe and kissed him on the cheek.

Before he could respond, she'd slipped out the door.

Joe's heart skipped a beat. For the first time since Lisa had said yes to his proposal, he felt real hope.

CHAPTER TWELVE

"OH, THIS IS CUTE," Shannon exclaimed.

Lisa studied the baby crib Shannon had ushered her toward.

"It's white, so it would work for a boy or a girl, right?" her friend suggested.

Lisa knew what she was doing. Shannon had wanted to cheer her up by suggesting this little shopping trip, but Lisa felt sure that wasn't going to happen.

She just couldn't find her way in this marriage. Nothing turned out right. She and Joe seemed to be constantly moving in different directions. They never connected.

Except on one level.

His desire for her physically was a palpable thing, as was hers for him.

But it wasn't supposed to be about sex only! Was it?

God, she didn't know anymore. She was so confused. There were moments when she could see just how good they would be together. Like last night, when they'd opened those gifts. But then reality would intrude. She'd kissed him, chastely, but a kiss all the same. A part of her had wanted them to go to bed together then and there, but by the time they'd cleaned up the wrapping paper, fear and confusion had taken hold once more.

Last night, she'd lain in bed and replayed every moment of their brief marriage. Then she'd considered their earlier relationship. Being together should be so easy, but it wasn't. Nothing was working out the way it should.

"It's great," she relented when Shannon continued to wait expectantly for her response to the crib. "White would be fine."

Shannon's enthusiastic smile drooped. "But it's not exactly what you want?"

Lisa felt like throwing up her hands in defeat. Instead, she braced her elbows on the crib rails. "I'm not sure what I want anymore." Her gaze connected with her friend's. "I really thought this was the right thing to do. That this baby needed both its mother and father. But the whole marriage situation feels strained." She shook her head. "Not a single thing has turned out the way I thought it would. Joe tries, I try, but somehow we fail to connect."

Shannon moved to her side and draped a comforting arm over her shoulders. "I know this is tough, but I think you guys can make it work."

Lisa shot her a dubious look. "You're my best friend. You're supposed to say that."

"Yeah, I know," Shannon admitted. "But I know both of you. The real problem is that you're perfect opposites. You're this conservative person who thinks through every decision, doesn't go jumping in without looking first. On the other hand, Joe dives in wherever he's needed. You can't be loaded with enough testosterone to face the risks Joe Ripani does every day on the job and not have some of it spill over into your personal life. I'm living proof of that and I'm not even a guy. He rubs you the wrong way with his confidence, his cocky, cavalier attitude toward life. You just have to find your equal ground, that's all."

Lisa knew there was a good deal of truth in what her friend said. Men like Joe would no doubt have a difficult time turning off that rush when the shift ended. Intellectually, she knew it took just that kind of drive and self-confidence to get the job done—to face the fire.

But it was pure hell being married to that kind of arrogance.

That wasn't fair. Joe had gone above and beyond to please her, yet somehow it always backfired. She couldn't deny his effort and determination. And she had fared no better. Whatever she attempted turned out the wrong way, too.

Maybe if they could both just relax and let things happen naturally, everything would work out. Heat slid through her at the thought of where that route would lead: straight to bed.

Her entire body ached for his touch. She wanted him so badly she'd begun to fantasize in the middle of the day about sex. Her mind replayed every magnificent second they'd enjoyed before.

Before the breakup…before the baby…and the wedding.

"Earth to Lisa," Shannon droned. "Come in, Lisa."

Lisa jerked back to attention, annoyed that she'd zoned out. "Sorry, what did you say?"

"I didn't meet you here to watch you stand around day-dreaming." Shannon chastised her with a knowing look.

Even her friend recognized what her problem was, Lisa realized. She'd asked Shannon to meet her for a bit of a selfish reason. She desperately did not want to hole up in her office or go home for lunch. Joe would be at home. She didn't want to face him. Not right now, anyway. She was too confused…too weak to fight the need to chuck all her lofty ideals and go for what she knew they did best. Thankfully, Shannon had suggested shopping, as well. Lisa needed to pick out nursery furnishings and accessories. She might as well take advantage of the distraction.

"Okay." Lisa considered the pristine white crib. "Not this one."

Forcing her attention to happier thoughts, she headed toward the array of lovely cherry and mahogany cribs. She stopped next to an intricately carved, richly stained cherry crib. "This is gorgeous." She ran her hand over the smooth finish. "This would be perfect."

There was a matching dresser and changing table. Excitement stirred Lisa's blood then. Her baby deserved the best. Taking care of her child's needs was something she could do right. "And this." She pointed to a big, comfortable-looking rocking chair. She sank onto the luxurious cushioned seat and pushed the rocker into motion. "Perfect."

Shannon grinned. "You look right at home. Are we buying today?"

She should come back with Joe and his truck, Lisa supposed. Besides, it wouldn't be fair not to ask his opinion. "I guess not." She stood. "We'll just check everything out and get an idea of what I need. Then Joe and I can come back and make the purchases."

Shannon wrapped her arm around Lisa's and guided her toward the bedding. "So what happened last night?" She started to laugh but tried to cover it by clearing her throat. "I...uh...heard that the poker game landed at your house."

Was everyone at the station talking about her marital problems? With all that was going on in the world today, there were certainly more pressing topics.

"They were smoking cigars," Lisa explained. "In the house. Secondhand smoke, you know?"

Shannon laughed outright then. "Sorry." She managed a fittingly outraged expression. "You're right. That's terrible. I heard Joe was a little startled by your reaction."

Lisa might as well fess up to the whole story. "I think I scared him." She glanced around to make sure no one would overhear. "He was so worried about how upset I got that he agreed to counseling."

"What?" Shannon looked absolutely flabbergasted. "I don't believe it."

"Shannon," Lisa scolded, "that's not fair. He's really

trying to make this work. For a little while last night, we connected on a level that had nothing to do with...well, you know."

"Okay, okay. I know." She stopped at a display and checked out the colorful comforters decorated with cartoon characters. "It's just that I can't help getting a kick out of his misery. He's had this coming for weeks now. Ever since he broke up with you."

Misery.

That's what this marriage was for him, Lisa realized with sudden blinding clarity. Joe hadn't really wanted to get married. He'd admitted as much. He wasn't the marrying kind. She had known that up front, and yet she'd gone along with this harebrained idea.

"Uh-oh." Shannon was staring at her as if anticipating some sort of complete meltdown. "I didn't mean it that way."

"You're right." Lisa breathed the words, scarcely able to dredge up the necessary energy to push them past her lips. "He is miserable. So am I." That's why those special moments were so few and far between.

"I'm sorry, Lisa. I shouldn't have said that." Shannon looked really worried now. "Let's pick out a cute comforter. Something that doesn't have wacky characters all over it. Come on." She dragged Lisa deeper into the store's baby department, which was filled with lace and frills and every color imaginable.

Lisa pretended to be interested, but nothing could divert her attention from the single word that so very accurately described this marriage.

Misery.

Joe would grow bitter all right. Before long, even the physical attraction would fade and then he would hate her.

How could she do that to him?

To herself?

IT WAS HIS DAY OFF, and what was he doing?

Grocery shopping.

Joe tossed a couple more cans of soup into the cart. The fridge and cupboards were still half-empty, leaving him no choice but to stock them. Admittedly, Lisa had picked up a few supplies. She'd told him that cooking for one had always seemed a waste so she hadn't bothered much when she lived alone. But now they were together and he wanted to do this the right way. He wanted to stock their kitchen and do a little cooking. He could survive without dropping by the Bar and Grill for a few days. Besides, he'd had all the ribbing he could take about Seaborn's lucky shot.

The shiner had gone from black to a nasty purple and green.

Truth be told, Joe felt damn green on the inside.

At five-thirty this afternoon, they had an appointment with Dr. Serena Carlisle, marriage counselor. He groaned. He did not want to discuss his marital problems—specifically his lack of a sex life—with some stranger.

He wanted Lisa to be happy, but he'd just about decided that might be impossible.

He'd done everything he knew how to do, and nothing was right—absolutely nothing. Well, there had been a moment last night. Why couldn't it be like that all the time? Why couldn't they just enjoy each other?

At this point he was embarrassed to ask his brothers or his buddies for advice. He'd been married a week and already he was afraid to make even the slightest wrong move.

Surely it wasn't supposed to be this way.

Doubt weighed heavily on his shoulders.

Enough feeling sorry for yourself, he railed. It wasn't as if this was easy for Lisa, either.

They just had to find common ground. From what he'd been told, every couple had problems adapting at first. A marriage couldn't grow without growing pains, right?

He wasn't ready to give up just yet. Not for one second would he admit defeat. Not with a guy like Seaborn waiting in the wings for just such an opportunity.

Fury kindled in his gut. No way.

Lisa was his. The baby was his.

He wasn't giving up on anything. Not now. Not ever.

He would make this marriage work if it killed him.

Shoving the cart down the aisle, he tossed at least two of each item he thought they could use into the basket. He didn't know jack about grocery shopping for Lisa, since he didn't have a good grasp of her likes and dislikes just yet, but she would have to give him points for effort.

He would cook and clean and shop until she admitted that he was the best husband a woman could want.

Until she threw herself into his arms and begged him to take her to bed.

A need so urgent that it took his breath away stopped Joe in his tracks. Lisa was worth the wait and the effort.

He cared a great deal for her…for their child.

He would make this work.

AS DETERMINED AS Joe was, he almost faltered when faced with the marriage counselor's advice.

"You want us to what?" he asked, almost choking on the words.

Lisa looked as mortified as he did.

"The courtship ritual," Dr. Carlisle repeated. "It's a crucial part of the bonding process. You cannot move forward as a couple until you've made all the proper connections on all the necessary levels. As far as I can tell, the one common link thus far has been purely physical."

Well, duh, Joe thought. It didn't take a psychology degree to figure that one out.

"That's a start," the doctor allowed.

"What, exactly, do we do?" Lisa asked cautiously.

"Go out to dinner. Hold hands. Talk about your likes and dislikes. The same things you probably did on your first date."

Joe's gaze met Lisa's and they instantly looked away from each other. They hadn't done much talking…not even on their first date. Things had gone from hello to hotter than Hades in mere minutes.

"Start tonight," Dr. Carlisle encouraged. "Take Lisa out to a nice restaurant," she said to Joe. "Go to a movie afterward. Something warm and romantic. When you get home, try giving each other a massage. I have videotapes for instruction."

When they left the counselor's office, videos and pamphlets in hand, Joe tried to think of something witty to say, but nothing came.

After he'd settled Lisa into the passenger seat of his truck, he skirted the hood and climbed in behind the wheel. He tossed the bag of goodies into the back seat.

A kind of numbness had set in on him, and from Lisa's expression, she suffered the same.

What the hell were they going to do?

Everybody had advice, but none of it felt right.

"So," he ventured, "where would you like to have dinner?" In a flash, an image of his well-stocked kitchen zipped through his mind. The fridge was full of milk, juice, cheese, meat and other fresh items. He'd even picked up an assortment of fruit. He'd read that it was good for the mother-to-be and the baby.

But the doc had said to go out to dinner. A date.

"Wherever you'd like to go is fine with me."

Well, that was a lot of help.

He pulled out onto the street. "How about John Paul's?" It was French, ritzy and cost an arm and a leg. Surely that would be acceptable. They'd missed having dinner there after the wedding. Seemed like a good place to start.

"Don't we need a reservation?"

"I know someone who works there. Maybe he can get us in without one."

Joe's friend came through. They only had to wait about twenty minutes.

LISA WASN'T SURE what she had expected from a marriage counselor, but somehow this wasn't it. She'd wanted someone to tell her what the problem was and how to go about fixing it. Prescribing a courtship ritual definitely wasn't what she'd anticipated. Not that she had an actual problem with it, but it seemed a waste of time.

Didn't they need to talk? To work out their issues so they could move forward? What good would dinner and a movie do?

She didn't need anyone to tell her where the massage would lead.

But then why torture herself like this? Why not just jump into the sack with him and be done with it! At least they would have some kind of intimacy in common. Some sort of link.

She felt like a stranger sitting here with Joe. Two strangers thrust into an unbearable situation without a thing in common.

Talk about something…anything. Tell him what you did today, a little voice urged.

"Shannon and I went shopping for nursery furniture and accessories today," she said, her voice far too perky.

"Really?" Joe's interest looked every bit as forced as her own. "Did you pick anything out?"

She thought about that. "Yes." She nodded thoughtfully. "I saw a lot I liked. Maybe we can go on the weekend—pick up a few things. I'd like to paint the second bedroom and get everything into place before physical activity becomes limited."

There she went, making all the decisions. Not to

mention that the term *physical activity* seemed to depress Joe all the more. "Unless you'd rather look somewhere else first," she said. "You might have something in mind already."

He waved off the suggestion. "No. Whatever you picked out will be fine."

Did that mean he wasn't interested?

"Okay." The baby had to have a room, Lisa assured herself. Whether or not Joe got excited about the decor didn't change the bottom line.

"How were things at the clinic today?"

Lisa looked up from the stemmed glass she'd been fingering. Did he really care how her day had gone, or was he just following the doctor's orders?

Did it even matter?

"Great." She shrugged. "We're really busy like always. Just routine procedures today—no emergencies or unexpected surgeries."

Silence fell. What did she say now? Technically it was her turn to keep the conversation going.

"What did you do today?" The question lacked originality but at least it filled the gap.

"I went to the store and stocked up on food."

"Really? I should have gotten more the other day, but I wasn't sure what you wanted."

"I tried to pick up a wide selection so I'd be sure and get items you liked, too."

How sweet. The thoughtfulness of the gesture made her smile. "Thanks."

Wow. Joe shopped. Who knew? Come to think of it,

he'd been doing laundry and dishes, as well. He really was working at this. "I appreciate all the things you've been doing around the house. I don't know where my head has been."

He smiled. "I don't mind."

Her tummy did a funny little flip-flop, and warmth spread through her. She appreciated that he'd taken the initiative.

"Would you like to go to a movie after dinner?" he asked.

The waiter's arrival postponed her answer.

Lisa took the waiter's suggestion of grilled salmon since she hadn't gotten around to viewing the menu. Joe did the same.

"I've been thinking that you should consider buying a new car," he said when the waiter had left.

She needed to do that. It surprised her that Joe had even bothered to think about it. "I guess I should."

"I'll be glad to help you pick something out, if you'd like."

"That would be nice."

He smiled, and she did the same.

Things only got better from there.

They chatted about everything from the weather to the latest reports of mild aftershocks related to the quake that had crumpled the parking garage. It felt good just to be with Joe. Maybe the counselor was right about what they needed. At two hundred bucks an hour, she ought to be, Lisa mused.

She and Joe had decided to see a romantic comedy

after dinner. Again, she was surprised that he hadn't wanted to head straight home and try out the massage video. She had to admit that going along with the counseling was above and beyond the call for him. Maybe she should go the full distance, as well.

It wasn't as if she didn't want to have sex as much as he did. Why fight it any longer? It was only making them both miserable.

They had to find common ground someplace. It might as well be a place they both could enjoy.

Lisa's courage rallied. She refused to let this misery eat at her—or Joe—a moment longer. Things were going to be different from now on.

JOE FELT GREATLY RELIEVED that Lisa appeared to be enjoying their *date*. Though he'd thought the whole idea was ridiculous when the counselor first suggested the courtship thing, he had to admit that it might just work.

He'd always been good at dating. All he had to do was relax and let things flow naturally. A part of him was already primed for the massage part. On one level, it seemed a little foolish to get so excited over the prospect of sharing such a superficial intimacy with his wife, but on another level—the one that had been starving for attention—it felt damn right.

He couldn't wait to get Lisa home. But first he had to sit through the movie. A grin slid across his face. He remembered soft whispers and holding hands in the dark. The movie idea could turn out to be more stimulating than the dinner.

The evening was going more smoothly than he could ever have anticipated. Lisa talked about her plans for the nursery and seemed to come alive right before his eyes as she told him about turning his backyard into a retreat for their child, as well as the animals she took in from time to time.

Joe let her talk. He didn't want to say or do anything that would slow the momentum. He loved listening to her voice and watching how animated she became. He couldn't help remembering that she was very much like that in bed. More than once he caught men in the restaurant staring at his beautiful wife. His chest swelled with pride. She was his.

Tonight…if he was damn lucky…he intended to show her how grateful he was to have her.

BY THE TIME Joe pulled into the driveway after the movie, he felt like a new man. Holding hands with Lisa in the dark theater, nuzzling her ear each time he whispered to her, just sitting next to her had his entire body humming with anticipation. That she was equally affected made the whole night a success. Maybe they'd finally hit their stride.

He unlocked the front door and allowed her to go in ahead of him.

She tossed her sweater onto the back of the sofa. "Would you like to watch the video now?"

For one long beat he couldn't answer. He could only

stare at her and be amazed all over again at just how beautiful she was. The navy blue sheath fit her like a glove. The hem, just a few inches above her knees, showed off those toned legs, and he wanted nothing more than to kiss her from ankle to hip.

"I don't think I'll need any video." He moved up behind her and started to knead her shoulders. "I think we can figure this out on our own," he whispered against her ear.

She made a soft sound and leaned against him. "I think you're right."

Taking that as his cue, he swept her silky hair aside and kissed her neck as he'd longed to do for days. She tasted so good. His arms slid around her waist and he pulled her more firmly against him. He groaned at the feel of her nicely rounded bottom pressing into his throbbing loins.

"Lisa, I want you so much," he murmured, nuzzling her satiny skin.

"Joe." His name was a mere whimper, a wanton breath on her lips.

His hand slid up to her breast and she gasped at his touch. His body reacted in kind, hardening like granite at the lush firmness of her breast, despite the layers of fabric separating them.

"Oh, God!"

Lisa jerked out of his arms and ran toward the bedroom.

Joe just stood there for several seconds, dumbfounded. The bathroom door slammed and he blinked.

What the hell had just happened?

He'd thought they were headed toward the bedroom, all right, but not quite at a dead run.

When he'd regained full control of his senses, he walked up to the bathroom door and tapped softly on it. "Lisa, are you okay?"

"I—"

He frowned as what sounded like some serious up-chucking interrupted whatever she'd intended to say.

Nausea.

Damn.

He'd read about that, too. Morning sickness didn't always occur in the morning.

"Can I get you anything?" he offered, feeling awkward and helpless. He'd never stood in the hall and listened to a woman lose her lunch—or dinner, as it were. It didn't sound fun. He grimaced.

"No!" She uttered the word breathlessly. "Just…go away. Okay? Please."

He frowned. Surely he could do something to make her feel better. Another round of heaving pretty much ruled out that possibility. Shaking his head in defeat, he wandered from the room.

Talk about bad timing. Just when things had started to look up.

No way would they be able to recapture the mood, he thought, plopping down on the sofa. Not that he could blame her.

But it really did suck.

He reached for the remote and clicked on the sports channel just in time to hear the commentator relate that a hockey player from his favorite team had gotten injured and would be out for the rest of the season.

Joe pumped up the volume a notch. He wanted to hear this. Misery loved company, and he damn sure needed some company right now.

CHAPTER THIRTEEN

JOE COULDN'T TAKE it anymore.

If just one more of his buddies waltzed up and bemoaned the fact that married guys had it made, he was going to detonate like a couple dozen grenades.

He had it made, all right. Made all the way to hell, only there didn't appear to be any way back. He felt ready to pull out his hair!

When Lisa had finally come out of the bathroom last night, while he'd ducked into the kitchen for a snack, she'd gone straight to bed without even saying good-night.

The meager little kisses he'd gotten to bestow upon her before the bout of nausea had done nothing but drive him closer to the edge. He'd had to take a late-night run just to get any sleep.

This was damned ridiculous.

When he'd left for work at 5:00 a.m. this morning, she'd still been asleep. He couldn't bring himself to disturb her, even though he'd wanted to say goodbye.

When he'd arrived at the firehouse, some of the guys going off duty were still hanging around, and Joe couldn't be sure if they had started a discussion on the fringe benefits of marriage to goad him or if they were serious. They couldn't know what was going on in his house.

His whole perspective was skewed. This entire thing made about as much sense as a book written backward.

It didn't help that his stomach roiled as if he'd been on a weekend drinking binge. Keeping down the breakfast he'd picked up at the Bar and Grill seemed less likely all the time.

What the hell was wrong with him?

Everything felt out of sync.

Marriage was supposed to be about compromise. About partnership. Hadn't his brothers told him that? Where had he gone wrong? Even nature was against him, case in point the untimely appearance of morning sickness. What did he do now?

If he compromised any further, he'd cease to exist.

For the first time since he'd said, "I do," Joe wished he'd never proposed and taken that fateful walk down the aisle.

Guilt pinged his conscience but he couldn't help it. How the hell was he supposed to feel? He wasn't blaming Lisa. She was suffering as much as he was.

From the moment he'd decided to propose, he'd put his old life behind him and hadn't given a second thought to the way things used to be. Well, okay, he had thought about the sex. A lot. But for the most part, he hadn't looked back.

Well, he was damn sure looking back now.

He wanted his life back, his old one. The one where he felt he had the world by the tail.

If being a husband and father-to-be was this much trouble, why did anybody do it? He almost laughed out loud. Because they didn't know that in advance, idiot, he answered himself. By the time a guy discovered the truth, it was too late.

Just like it was for him.

Too damn late for regrets.

Too damn late for anything but more confusion and misery.

He should write a self-help book of his own—*Marriage: The Real Story.*

Maybe Lisa had been right. Maybe guys like him just weren't cut out for marriage.

LISA WALKED all the way around the shiny new SUV. "Wow," she said. It was beautiful.

"Has all the latest safety features," the salesman commented.

He'd hovered around Lisa from the moment she entered the lot. She hated the hassle of buying a car, but she couldn't keep the rental forever. The salesman had been tracking her every move, as if he feared her business would be snatched up by one of the other sales reps hanging around the dealership lobby. This sort of business was more than likely dog-eat-dog, survival of the fittest.

The memory of Joe saying that he would help her buy a new car nudged at her, but she pushed it away. She didn't want to talk to him today. Didn't want to see the disappointment in his eyes all over again. She'd bought her last vehicle without any help. She could buy this one the same way.

As she stared at the car's well-equipped interior, she considered that last night had been the most humiliating experience of her life. She'd been ready to be intimate with Joe. And then her first bout of morning sickness had hit. She'd puked, he'd stood in the hall and listened. So much for romance. How was she supposed to feel sexy after that?

How pathetic could she get?

No amount of brushing her teeth and gargling with mouthwash had gotten rid of the horrible taste in her throat.

It just wasn't fair. She had reveled in his touch, loved the feel of his kisses against her skin, and what had she done? Almost barfed on his shoes.

Humiliation burned on her cheeks even now.

Though the sudden wave of nausea was related to pregnancy, still it was embarrassing. She hoped Joe hadn't taken her reaction personally. She'd wanted to explain but hadn't been able to face him afterward. And he'd left for work already when she awoke that morning.

How would she ever make up for it?

"Would you like to take her for a test drive?"

Lisa smoothed a hand over the luxurious leather seats and sighed. The SUV was big, beautiful and met stringent safety standards. She loved it.

That it was bright red made it a little out of character for her, but she was ready for some changes in her life.

Good changes.

She'd had all the painful ones she could endure. She'd played by some silly set of rules for far too long. Those standards no longer fit. She wasn't her mother or her sister.

"Why not?" she said to the salesman, who was no doubt calculating his commission at that very second.

If she was going to turn over a new leaf, she had to start somewhere. A wonderful idea struck her just then. She should pick up some new, sexy lingerie, as well. To make up for last night. Joe had to be thoroughly frustrated.

Lisa was sick to death of misunderstandings and tension-filled moments. The only kind of tension she wanted to feel between them from now on was the sexual kind.

LESS THAN ONE HOUR LATER, Lisa had herself a brand-new SUV. The salesman, who'd just made his quota for the week, had offered to drive her rental car back to the leasing agency.

Her next purchase took almost as much time as buying the car. She'd scoured the lingerie boutique for the most feminine undergarments she could find, then she'd called Greg and taken the rest of the afternoon off.

She had big plans for tonight.

As she fingered the silky teddy she'd selected, a smile teased her lips. Just thinking about Joe touching her while she was wearing nothing but the teddy almost made her melt on the spot.

She was way past ready for this night, and he was, too.

Maybe she'd drop by the firehouse and surprise him, Lisa thought as she made her way to the counter. It was likely too late for lunch, but she could apologize for last night. Even though the bout of nausea had embarrassed her, she should have said good-night before hiding in the bedroom.

She wasn't going to let this fester between them any longer. In fact, she intended to give Joe something to think about the rest of the day.

Anticipation making her giddy, she quickly paid for her merchandise and hurried out to her new candy-apple-red SUV.

She loved it.

Loved her new sexy lingerie.

Loved her even sexier husband.

Whether he loved her or not, she was going to be the best wife ever. Their child would never have to wonder if his or her parents truly loved each other. Maybe her love could be strong enough for both of them. She could do this. Their marriage didn't have to be perfect, it just had to be something they both enjoyed. Their current misery wasn't getting them anywhere.

Lisa backed out of the parking slot and pulled out onto the street. The firehouse wasn't far from here. After stopping by to see Joe, she would go home and cook something spectacular. Tonight they would feast in their cozy home and then they'd make a romance movie of their own.

The next few moments happened so fast that Lisa didn't have time to be afraid.

The ground shook hard, startling a gasp from her. It must be an aftershock from the quake she'd survived just days ago, she surmised in the next instant.

Instinctively her fingers clenched the steering wheel. Just as suddenly, her eyes widened with disbelief. She tried to cut to the right, but it was too late.

The car in the oncoming lane was headed right toward her.

The sound of crumpling metal and breaking glass was the last thing she heard.

"RIPANI!"

Joe looked up at the sound of O'Shea's voice. He frowned at the interruption. He'd stolen away from the others to make a call in private. He wanted to check on Lisa.

He couldn't bear the strain of not knowing if she was okay or not. There could be more going on than mere morning sickness. He should check on her.

Maybe it was stupid. But that little aftershock that had made the ground tremble for about ten seconds had him thinking about the quake. About how he'd almost lost her that day…and the baby. Apparently the aftershock hadn't been bad enough to cause any real trouble, but it made him think about how short life could be.

"Ripani!"

"What?" he growled as he slammed down the receiver. Couldn't a guy make a phone call without being hunted down?

O'Shea stopped in the doorway of the office. One look at her set his senses on full alert. Her eyes were glassy with fear. Her lips trembled. What the hell? O'Shea wasn't one to show emotion. What was wrong with her?

"You need to come with me," she said, her voice quavering.

Joe pushed up from his chair and stood toe-to-toe with her. "What the hell's going on, O'Shea?" Fear had started pounding in the back of his brain. He didn't want to hear the answer to that question. He had no idea what had happened, but every instinct warned that it wasn't good, and that it had something to do with—

"Lisa's been in an accident. The aftershock...another car hit her head-on. I don't know how bad it is, but we gotta get to the hospital now."

It took ten damn minutes to get to the hospital.

The tremor had caused two more accidents, nothing major, but enough congestion to stall traffic between the firehouse and the hospital.

Joe kept imagining Lisa in that little rental car. A head-on collision. That was bad. Why the hell hadn't he insisted she pick out something new before now? Something big and safe like the SUV she'd lost in the parking garage?

Now it was too late.

The realization that he'd almost had his selfish wish come true hit him like a runaway dump truck.

He'd wished he had his old life back.

He'd regretted the marriage...

"Oh, God," he murmured on a wave of pain that brought tears to his eyes.

O'Shea said nothing. She just drove. Joe knew she was hurting, too. Lisa was her best friend.

The baby.

Another tide of agony washed over him.

What if she lost the baby?

Joe was out of the vehicle before it had completely stopped in the E.R. parking lot. He raced toward the building, O'Shea right behind him.

"Lisa Ripani," he demanded of the woman behind the desk. "Where is she?"

"Calm down, sir," the admitting nurse, one he didn't recognize, cautioned. "The doctor's in with her now. It'll be a few minutes before—"

"Where?" he roared. "I'm her husband. I want to know where she is! Now!"

O'Shea stepped in. "Is there any way he can be with her?"

"I'm afraid not," she said with genuine sympathy. "Dr. Metcalf is an OB. Mr. Ripani can go in when the doctor's finished his exam."

Joe prayed that calling in an OB was just routine procedure and not because there was a problem with the baby.

O'Shea thanked the woman behind the desk and pushed him toward a chair, but he couldn't sit down.

"Come on, Ripani, sit down. Save your energy for when you get in there."

She wilted into the molded plastic and Joe forced himself to take the seat beside her. His heart raced but couldn't seem to beat quickly or efficiently enough to provide him with the oxygen he needed. Panic, he told himself. He knew the symptoms.

For the first time since he'd stormed in here, he noticed the other people in the room. Not that many, thankfully. None who appeared to be badly injured.

And then he began to pray.

He prayed for Lisa and the baby.

He prayed for the strength and the knowledge to do the right thing, to be a better husband.

He prayed for one more chance.

"MR. RIPANI."

Joe shot to his feet and rushed toward the doctor, who waited near the "authorized personnel only" doors. O'Shea lagged behind him, but close enough to hear the news.

"How's Lisa?" Joe's voice felt weak. Hell, he felt weak all over.

"She's going to be fine, Mr. Ripani. It was the baby we were most concerned about."

The realization that he'd waited only half an hour— though it had felt like a lifetime—sank fully into Joe's brain. "Is the baby okay?"

"Yes. Everything is fine. There was some abdominal cramping when she first arrived, so we had to run a few tests to make sure the pregnancy was still viable."

Joe nodded, his relief making it hard to concentrate. "Can I see her now?"

"Sure." The doctor glanced past him at O'Shea. "One at a time, though. She's pretty shaken and I'd like to keep the excitement level as low as possible. We'll be admitting her for overnight observation."

Joe glanced back at O'Shea. "Go," she told him. "You tell her I'm here."

Joe managed a jerky nod before following the doctor down the corridor beyond the double doors. The medicinal smell of the hospital made Joe feel nauseated. Thank God Lisa was all right. Thank God. That was the only thought he could manage to process.

At the door of the treatment room, the doctor hesitated. "Remember, we want to keep her calm."

"Calm," Joe repeated. His own heart pounded, but he had to look calm...had to stay calm. Not overreact.

The doctor opened the door and Joe stepped inside.

Lisa lay on the treatment table, a white sheet stretched over the lower part of her body. Her blouse was bloody.

Joe's knees threatened to buckle beneath him.

Where the hell was that iceman persona right now?

Upon closer inspection, he realized the blood had come from a cut on her forehead. The doctor had already made the necessary repair with tiny butterfly tapes. It didn't look too bad, but head injuries always bled profusely.

"Hey," he whispered.

Her blue eyes were bright with tears and he barely made it the rest of the way to her side without doubling over at the emotion wrenching his gut.

"They said the baby is fine," she told him, her voice trembling.

"That's right. But they want you to hang around overnight to make sure you stay nice and calm. Keep an eye on things. That okay?"

She moved her head in a respectable attempt at a nod. "I wrecked my new car."

Confusion made his head throb. "What new car?"

"I did a little shopping," she said, her fingers smoothing the wrinkles on the sheet draped over her abdomen. "I bought a new SUV." She glanced at him. "It's pretty beat up now."

"We'll take care of it or get you another one," he assured her with a smile. Damn, he was glad she hadn't been in that dinky rental.

"I was scared, Joe." She looked directly into his eyes, tears spilling past her lashes. "Really scared. I thought I was going to lose the baby, but the doctor said the cramps were likely related to the emotional stress of the accident."

Joe's jaw hardened at the idea that the other stress they'd been going through might have been to blame, as well.

"It's okay now. Everything's okay."

"I'm sorry about last night." Her breath caught on the last word.

It was all he could do not to grab her and hold her, but he resisted the impulse. He had to be careful not to upset her. "No big deal. We'll have lots more nights to make up for lost time." He smiled and took her hand in his. "I think I suffered a little morning sickness myself." His other hand went to his gut. "It was all I could do to hang on to my breakfast."

That coaxed a smile from her.

He kissed her forehead—he couldn't help himself. He had to. "We'll be fine, Lisa. I promise."

She touched his face before he could draw back, and caressed his jaw. He swallowed hard at the emotions welling in him. He wanted to kiss her lips to show her how much she meant to him, but he couldn't. Couldn't do anything to upset her in any way.

Lisa started to say something, but the door swung inward before she had a chance.

"Okay, Ms. Ripani, time to move you to a room."

Joe squeezed her hand. "I'll be right behind you. Shannon's here. She'll be in to see you, too."

The nurse glanced over at him. "We'll be taking her up to 412. Why don't you take care of the paperwork at the desk and then you and your friend can visit her in her room."

"Sure thing." He wiggled his fingers at his wife and moved out into the corridor.

Several seconds passed before he could walk back to the lobby. He had to pull himself together first—wipe the dampness from his face. Apparently the Iceman was melting.

He'd almost lost her…again.

God had given him yet another chance to prove what he was made of. This time he wasn't going to screw it up.

CHAPTER FOURTEEN

LISA AWAKENED slowly the next morning. Every muscle in her body screamed in protest at being disturbed from slumber, and her mouth felt as dry as the Mojave.

She moaned and rolled onto her side. An ache split across her forehead…

Then she remembered.

The tremor.

The other vehicle coming toward her.

Fear slid through her and her hand went automatically to her abdomen. She was in the hospital. The baby was fine. Everything was fine.

Lisa heaved a ragged sigh of relief. Thank God.

Joe.

She turned her head to see if he was still in the chair next to her bed. But it was Shannon who sat dozing there.

Lisa was glad to see her friend, but where was Joe?

He'd been there when she went to sleep. Later, when she'd awakened, Shannon had told her he'd stepped out for a bit. To take care of business, she'd said. Lisa had assumed that meant firefighting business. Her family had appeared about the same time but hadn't stayed long. Shannon had probably told them that the doctor wanted to limit Lisa's visitors.

Joe had returned, hovering around her bed like a mother hen, as if she was all that mattered to him in the universe. She couldn't say she hadn't enjoyed the attention, though it felt a little odd coming from Joe. It was true that he'd been more attentive in the past couple of weeks than she'd expected, but this went well beyond that. It was as if he was afraid that if he didn't take care of every little thing, didn't cater to her every whim, something disastrous would happen.

The behavior was just so out of character for the big guy. And the second time she'd awakened and found him sitting in the chair, he'd looked beat. She'd never seen him like that.

Joe Ripani was the Energizer Bunny, the Iceman. Nothing ever got to him or slowed him down.

Was his new haggard demeanor her doing?

She thought about the sexy lingerie she'd purchased yesterday and the big plans she'd had for her husband. It almost felt as if fate itself was against them. No matter what either of them did to try to make this marriage work, it always failed.

The sting of emotion burned her eyes. Were those cramps she'd suffered after the crash a foreshadowing of things to come? She squeezed her eyes shut and prayed that God would protect her baby from whatever bad karma she and Joe appeared to be plagued by. Her bleary gaze moved around the stark white room. She didn't want to be here. She didn't want to be sick. She wanted to be safe and happy and get back to work. Her mother had promised to call Greg and let him know what had happened. He'd probably drop by today. She felt terrible that she'd failed to do her part at the clinic lately. Somehow, some way she'd have to make that right.

"You're awake."

Shannon's voice dragged Lisa from her troubling thoughts. She managed a wan smile. "Awake and aching like someone took a baseball bat to me while I slept."

Shannon nodded knowingly. "The doc said you'd probably have bruises from the seat belt. That's typical, though. You'll be okay. Your new car is a whole other story," she added with a wry twist of her lips.

Lisa uttered another sigh and stared at the ceiling. "Great."

"Love the color, though," Shannon said. "Also loved the goodies I found in there." She waggled her eyebrows. "Had a hot date planned for last night, or do you always wear such skimpy underclothes?"

"I can't believe you went through my stuff," Lisa protested.

"It was either me or the cop who finalized the report. Had to make sure you weren't transporting any drugs or anything. You should have seen him blush when I pulled that one teddy out—"

"Shannon!"

"I'm kidding. Chill. I merely took your personal belongings from the vehicle before it was hauled away to the repair shop. That's all. No one saw those wicked undies but me. I wouldn't have even seen them if the contents of the bag hadn't spilled out all over the seat."

Lisa shook her head, then winced and reached for the bandage on her forehead. "You're sure no one else saw them?"

"Not a soul." Shannon picked up the pitcher on the table next to Lisa's bed and shook it. "You want something to drink? Breakfast? The nurse came by earlier but didn't want to wake you. She left a tray over there."

A covered cafeteria tray sat on a table on the far side of the room. Though she hadn't spent much time in hospitals, Lisa had heard stories about the food. "Does it look and smell palatable?"

Shannon shrugged. "I wouldn't eat it. Looks a little scary to me. Smells okay. The juice and the toast should be safe enough."

Juice and toast would be better than nothing. She had to eat something. She couldn't be sure what time the doctor would release her.

"Where's Joe?" she asked as nonchalantly as possible.

Shannon considered the question before answering. Panic instantly rippled through Lisa. Maybe he'd decided she and this baby were just too much trouble.

No, she reminded herself. Not Joe. He would never say die. No matter how unhappy he was, he wouldn't walk away from his child.

"To be honest," Shannon said, "I don't know where he is. He called and asked me to come stay with you about ten last night. He's been gone ever since. The nurse said he called the desk every hour or so all night."

Lisa had failed to give Joe the benefit of the doubt too often already. Wherever he was, he had his reasons for not being here. She had to believe that.

Or cry.

And she'd cried about all she could tolerate lately. Besides, her head hurt too much to cry.

"How 'bout that toast?" Shannon rolled the table over to the bed. "If we put enough jelly on it, it'll be edible."

WHEN JOE RETURNED to Lisa's room to take her home, he found O'Shea force-feeding hospital food to her. That was just like O'Shea. She took her job seriously, whether it was fighting fires or caring for a friend.

"Good morning, ladies."

Lisa's gaze flew to him, her blue eyes filled with relief. She was glad to see him. That one look made him want to clear the room and climb into that bed with her. But he couldn't do that. She was off limits for now. No excitement. Take it slow. He'd repeated those rules over and over again all night long.

O'Shea, on the other hand, looked anything but glad to see him. "What kept you?" she griped, eyeing him suspiciously. She was sharp. She knew he was up to something, and she didn't like being left out.

"I had business."

"In the middle of the night?" she grumbled good-naturedly, then waved her hand as if to erase the question. "Forget I asked."

"Already forgotten." He moved up to the other side of the bed and placed a gentle kiss just above the small bandage on Lisa's forehead. "You feeling okay this morning?"

"Fine," she said quickly. "Do you think they'll let me go home now?"

Home.

A smile kicked up one corner of his mouth. "Definitely. Doc said I could take you home anytime now."

Shannon pushed away the table holding the food tray. "I'm out of here, then." She gave Lisa's hand a pat. "Call me if you need me."

Lisa assured her she would, and Joe gave her a little salute of appreciation. O'Shea was a loyal squad member and friend, he admitted. He wouldn't forget all she'd done for Lisa.

And for him.

"You ready?"

"Past ready," Lisa confessed.

Before they could get going, the doctor waylaid them, making a last-minute appearance and deciding to check Lisa out once more. Joe didn't have a problem with that. Lisa was anxious to leave, but he would rather be sure all was as it should be. When he'd finished, Dr. Metcalf announced that Lisa could resume all normal activities.

As if to slow their departure a few minutes more, the nurse insisted on transporting Lisa to the entrance lobby in a wheelchair. Hospital policy, she declared.

Finally, they were on their way. Joe couldn't wait to get Lisa home.

He had a very special surprise for her.

LISA FELT tremendously relieved, as if a weight had been lifted from her, as Joe parked in their driveway.

If life were fair, she wouldn't have to worry about another car crash for several decades to come. She was definitely due for a break.

"I have the rest of the day off," Joe told her as he unlocked the front door and stepped aside for her to enter their home. "And Greg has things at the clinic under control."

Greg? Not Seaborn? Had Joe actually spoken her partner's name without grinding his teeth?

"When did you talk to Greg?"

Joe ushered her inside. The instant the door was closed, an unrecognizable scent tickled her nose.

"He came by the hospital to see you yesterday afternoon but you were sleeping."

Her attention shifted back to Joe. "You talked to him?" She didn't mean to sound so startled but, after all, they were speaking about Greg.

Joe made a sound that could have been a laugh but sounded more like a strangled sigh. "Yes. We actually talked for several minutes without coming to blows." He shrugged. "We reached a kind of understanding. A truce."

"I can't believe it," Lisa said.

Taking her arm, Joe guided her toward the hall. "Well, it's true. You can ask him yourself when you go back to work."

Overwhelmed. Shocked. Neither word accurately described what she felt at the moment. Joe and Greg reaching a truce? Incredible.

"I have a little surprise for you," Joe said softly.

That smell teased her senses again. It wasn't strong, not even unpleasant, just unfamiliar.

"Another one?"

"Funny. Now close your eyes."

"What?" She looked up at Joe.

"Just close your eyes," he said more firmly.

"Okay, I'm closing my eyes." She did as he said, ignoring the anticipation clanging in her ears and along every nerve ending in her body. What kind of surprise did he have in mind? The pleasant feel of his arms around her made her want to play this game all day. She liked his strength, the warmth of his big body close to hers.

Moving slowly, he led her forward a few more steps then stopped. "Tell me what you think."

Lisa opened her eyes and almost stopped breathing.

It was beautiful.

Unbelievable.

"Joe, when did you do this? How did you know?"

He'd bought every single piece of nursery furniture she'd admired the other day, including the bedding and accessories. He'd even painted the room a pale mint green that coordinated perfectly with the tiny dots in the comforter. That was the smell she hadn't recognized.

"Shannon told me about your shopping trip. I wanted to do something special for you…and the baby."

She turned in his arms and stared into those dark, smoldering eyes. "Thank you. I can't tell you how much this means to me. It's…" She turned back to the gorgeous room. "It's more beautiful than I imagined." It was perfect. The perfect room for their child.

"I know I've made a lot of mistakes, Lisa," he said, "but I want this to work. Not just for the baby, but for us." He cupped her face in his big, capable hands. "I love you. I didn't understand exactly what that meant until I almost lost you for the second time."

She searched his eyes…uncertainty slowing her thundering heart. "Are you sure, Joe? I don't want you to say anything that you don't feel comfortable saying. I've decided that it's okay if you don't love me that way…. We'll still make it work."

"The thought of losing you makes my gut twist with agony. When I'm away from you too long I feel lost, as if I don't belong anymore. I just didn't know what it meant until yesterday. *I love you.*" When she still looked unsure, he added, "I guess you'll just have to take my word for it." He kissed her cheek and left a promise there. "For now."

She fisted her fingers into his shirt and pulled him closer. "Sorry, big guy, but I like my guarantees in a more tangible form."

His pupils flared at the implication. "The excitement might be too much. I…"

"Didn't you hear Dr. Metcalf? He said I could resume normal activities." She flashed him a wicked smile. "I can't think of a single thing more normal than a man making love to his wife."

"But—"

"I know I've been avoiding sex," she said, her expression turning serious once more as she interrupted what he was about to say. "You have to understand that I was afraid. I was so afraid we wouldn't have anything more in common. That we wouldn't connect on any other level. Our lovemaking was always so consuming. But more than anything, I was afraid of losing you. If I let myself love you too much and then I lost you, I wouldn't be able to bear it." She closed her eyes and shook her head, but then those beautiful eyes opened to him once more. "I almost let myself forget that you—everything about you—is the man I fell in love with." A shy smile teased her lips. "I should have trusted that you wouldn't take unnecessary risks. That you would always do the right thing for me and for our child."

Joe didn't need any further provocation. He swept Lisa into his arms and carried her to their bedroom. He struggled with his mounting desire, with the need pounding in his body, but somehow he managed to undress her slowly, revealing her exquisite body with painstaking care.

When she was completely nude, he stood back and admired her. "You are so beautiful."

She patted her tummy. "Not for long."

He shook his head at the remark. "You'll be even more beautiful then."

She suddenly looked embarrassed. "I had bought some special lingerie to wear…for you…for our first time as a married couple." Her slender hands fluttered nervously.

He opened the top drawer of the bureau. "You mean these slinky goods?"

Her eyes widened. "I thought—"

"O'Shea gave your things to me. Told me I'd better not open the bag, but I did." He grinned. "I like this the best." He pulled out the lacy teddy she'd picked just for him, then he tossed it back into the drawer. "But you don't need any of it. You're perfect just the way you are."

His words gave her courage, and Lisa undressed him every bit as slowly as he had done with her. His powerful body bore the undeniable marks of his trade. Old injuries from fires and dangerous rescues. That was just part of what made Joe Ripani a hero. A driven man. One who would risk everything to save a single life.

"I love you, Joe," she murmured as he lay down beside her on the quilt that had been in her family for two generations. Three if she counted the baby growing inside her.

"Yes, you do," he said with a wink. "But—" he bent down and nipped her lips with his teeth "—I love you more."

HE MADE LOVE TO HER with incredible patience and finesse. Lisa didn't know how he held out. It had been so, so long. They'd wanted each other so desperately. Yet he pleasured her relentlessly before allowing himself the final moment of completion. He kissed her skin, every inch. His hot, hungry mouth suckled her breasts until she cried out his name. And then he moved lower. Making her plead for him to bring her to completion...making her admit that there was no one else for her but him. That she was his alone.

He was the only one who could take her to this special place. And then he gave her what she'd begged for, plunging into her over and over until the fiery sensations sang through her veins, cresting and culminating in wave after wave of exquisite pleasure.

This was the man who loved her.

The father of her child.

In that final moment of utter clarity before he thrust into her one last time, she saw the truth of the words he'd said to her, and then release claimed him.

He loved her.

This was the way it should be.

When their breathing had slowed, Lisa rose up onto her elbow to look at her satisfied hero sprawled across the tangled covers. Her husband. She loved looking at him. They'd both gone through so much, especially Joe, waiting for her to trust her heart. Maybe she should show him how she felt once more…just to make sure he got it.

She smoothed her hand over his chest, reveling in the rich, masculine contours. Approval rumbled low in his throat like a primal mating challenge.

"That," he said huskily, "was definitely worth the wait."

He started to reach for her, but she pushed him back against the mattress. "You're right, Ripani." She moved up on all fours. He shivered in anticipation, sending a rush of intense need and delicious power through her. "And I think we need to make up for lost time."

She straddled his lean waist. "Starting right now," she purred as she sank onto his rigid shaft…

That's where the thinking stopped.

JOE HELD LISA'S HAND as Dr. Metcalf pointed out the baby's pulsing heartbeat on the ultrasound. His own heart kicked into warp speed. He smiled down at his wife and sheer happiness flooded him. Their child thrived inside her.

It was still too early to see much of anything else, but just looking at that heartbeat, hearing it, was treat enough.

"About eight weeks' gestation," the doctor commented. "Based on the date of your last cycle, I'd set the due date as early October."

Lisa's fingers tightened around Joe's. The time would fly. Soon they would hold this precious life in their arms.

The doctor reminded Lisa to take her vitamins and scheduled her next visit. Joe could hardly wait for the next ultrasound, although it wouldn't be for a while, the doctor had told them.

"Would you like to go somewhere for lunch?" Lisa asked as they loaded into her as-good-as-new SUV. The color still amazed him. It matched that sexy teddy she'd bought. Or maybe the teddy matched the car. Whatever the case, they both reflected his lovely wife's wicked side. As reserved and mild-mannered as Lisa Malloy Ripani appeared, she was a tiger in his arms. And he loved every minute of it.

"There's only one place I'd like to be right now," he told her bluntly.

Judging by the knowing gleam in her eyes, she needed no further elaboration.

They had this communication thing down to a science. Just as if they had been born to be together.

No force on earth would ever shake them apart.

Ordinary people. Extraordinary circumstances.
Meet a new generation of heroes—
the men and women of
Courage Bay Emergency Services.

CODE RED
A new Harlequin continuity series continues
March 2005 with
AFTERSHOCKS
By Nancy Warren

Earthquake aftershocks trap Mayor Patrick O'Shea
and his assistant Briana Bliss in an elevator.
But emergency services are stretched to the limit with
911 calls. The mayor and Briana wait.
And passions flare....

Here's a preview!

"PATRICK? BRIANA? You okay?" The strong clear female voice jerked Briana awake. She heard the welcome whirr of the generator and then the sound of thumping and banging.

As she lifted her head from Patrick's shoulder, which she'd used as a pillow, a sharp crick in her neck had her stifling a howl of pain. She rubbed her neck while Patrick squeezed her shoulder, then rose to his feet and moved toward the front of the elevator.

"Hey, Shannon!" he yelled. "Hope we didn't haul you out of bed for this."

"For that crack, you get to buy the coffee."

"Get us out of here and I'll buy you breakfast. Anything you want." He turned to Briana. "My sister, Shannon," he said, overly cheerful. "She's a truckie on Engine One. She's the best."

"Great," Briana said, equally hearty as she struggled to her feet.

Already the real world was close and awkwardness crowding in as they stood together listening to the noise indicating imminent rescue.

Suddenly Patrick pulled her to him and kissed her hot and hard.

He took her hands and held them loosely. She wished she could see his face, but even though the generator was thrumming, the elevator was still in darkness. "I'm going to have to give you your job back now. Are you sure you want it?"

Silence pressed against her chest. She understood what he was saying. The minute she accepted her job back, the affair ended.

She could leave the mayor's staff now that she had the tape, of course. But after tonight, she knew she'd never use it. No. What had happened between them had been as unexpected and bizarre as the aftershock that had trapped them in the elevator.

There'd been a lot of time in the night to think. She'd intended to tape Patrick making an inappropriate pass. She would say no, loud and clear, then record him trying to talk her into having sex. The reality was pretty much the opposite. Patrick had tried to say no and Briana had thrown herself at him. She knew her uncle believed Patrick had faked the evidence that destroyed Cecil's chances of ever becoming mayor. She'd believed it, too. Who else had anything to gain by publishing a doctored picture and leaking a bogus story? Now, however, she was beginning to wonder if Patrick had actually had anything to do with leaking false evidence against his rival. Maybe someone on his campaign team had done the deed. Possibly, they hadn't even told him.

Okay, it was a slim chance, but she'd just made love

with the man. She wanted him to be as decent as he'd seemed in the two months she'd worked for him.

One way or another, she'd find out who had blackened her uncle's name. If that person was Patrick, then she'd do what she had to do.

She owed her uncle her loyalty.

But after tonight, she felt she owed Patrick some, too.

"I can't stay fired," she told him with real regret. "You need me."

He touched her face, and she felt tenderness in his fingertips. "You have no idea how much," he said.

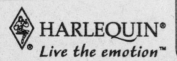

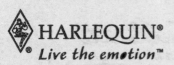

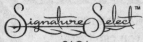

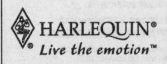

If you enjoyed what you just read,
then we've got an offer you can't resist!

Take 2 bestselling novels FREE!

Plus get a FREE surprise gift!

Clip this page and mail it to MIRA®

IN U.S.A.
3010 Walden Ave.
P.O. Box 1867
Buffalo, N.Y. 14240-1867

IN CANADA
P.O. Box 609
Fort Erie, Ontario
L2A 5X3

YES! Please send me 2 free MIRA® novels and my free surprise gift. After receiving them, if I don't wish to receive anymore, I can return the shipping statement marked cancel. If I don't cancel, I will receive 4 brand-new novels every month, before they're available in stores! In the U.S.A., bill me at the bargain price of $4.99 plus 25¢ shipping and handling per book and applicable sales tax, if any*. In Canada, bill me at the bargain price of $5.49 plus 25¢ shipping and handling per book and applicable taxes**. That's the complete price and a savings of over 20% off the cover prices—what a great deal! I understand that accepting the 2 free books and gift places me under no obligation ever to buy any books. I can always return a shipment and cancel at any time. Even if I never buy another The Best of the Best™ book, the 2 free books and gift are mine to keep forever.

185 MDN DZ7J
385 MDN DZ7K

Name	(PLEASE PRINT)	
Address	Apt.#	
City	State/Prov.	Zip/Postal Code

Not valid to current The Best of the Best™, Mira®,
suspense and romance subscribers.

Want to try two free books from another series?
Call 1-800-873-8635 or visit www.morefreebooks.com.

* Terms and prices subject to change without notice. Sales tax applicable in N.Y.
** Canadian residents will be charged applicable provincial taxes and GST.
   All orders subject to approval. Offer limited to one per household.
® and ™are registered trademarks owned and used by the trademark owner and or its licensee.

BOB04R   ©2004 Harlequin Enterprises Limited

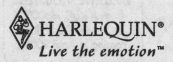

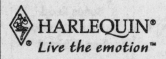